insight text guide

Robert Beardwood

# Selected Short Stories

## Henry Lawson

First published in 2002,
reprinted 2005, 2011,
reprinted with revisions in 2012, reprinted 2016, 2020 (twice), 2025.

Insight Publications Pty Ltd
3/350 Charman Road
Cheltenham VIC 3192
Australia
Tel: +61 3 8571 4950
Email: books@insightpublications.com.au

**www.insightpublications.com.au**



National Library of Australia Cataloguing-in-Publication entry:

Beardwood, Robert.
Selected stories, Henry Lawson.
For secondary and tertiary students.
ISBN 9781920693107
1. Lawson, Henry, 1867-1922 - Criticism and interpretation.
I. Title. (Series : Insight text guide).
A823.2

Other ISBNs:
9781922378972 (digital)

Cover design: The Modern Art Production Group

Printed by Markono Print Media Pte Ltd

# contents

## A note on the text

This text guide gives quotations and page references relevant to *The Penguin Henry Lawson Short Stories*, edited by John Barnes. Although page numbers obviously will vary according to the particular edition of the stories used, variations in the text will be slight.

# INTRODUCTION

Henry Lawson's short stories are some of the most famous and critically acclaimed in Australian literature. They were written during one of the most turbulent and pivotal times in Australian history: the 1890s and the early 1900s. This was the time of Federation, when the six self-governing colonies of the British Empire decided to come together, establishing the Australian nation on 1 January, 1901. Debates about the nature and future of Australian society were vigorous and diverse, and Australian writing and painting flourished as never before. It was also a time of hardship. The prosperous 1880s had given way to economic depression and a long, crippling drought in the 1890s. Many people who had been well-off suddenly became poor, and those in rural or outback regions had few certainties or comforts.

These stories reflect many aspects of Lawson's own times, and of the places and people he knew from personal experience. His accounts of bush and outback life in colonial Australia are a rich source of images and ideas about Australia's national identity. Lawson's distinctive, iconic characters have become part of the national mythology: the spirited, resourceful bushwoman in 'The Drover's Wife'; the larrikin bushman and raconteur, Jack Mitchell; the earnest and tender-hearted Joe Wilson; and the affectionate but misguided retriever in 'The Loaded Dog'.

Lawson's sympathies lie not with the aristocratic squatter but with the struggling selector and the indefatigable drover; in other words, with those of limited means who never shirk hard, physical work and never fail to help a mate. They are also with the wife and mother who raises the children, runs the family farm and survives floods, droughts, disease, loneliness and the inevitable drunk or desperate 'sundowner'. Lawson's characters have a dry but indomitable sense of humour. They are practical and realistic, compassionate but with little tolerance for the sentimental or romantic.

The characters in these stories gain much of their dignity, and their enduring presence in Australian culture, from their willingness to treat their fellow men and women as their equals. This is known as the egalitarian bush ethos, and even in contemporary, cosmopolitan Australia it continues to be invoked and celebrated. However mythical it may be, the spirit of bush egalitarianism and the associated masculine ideal of mateship are at their most recognisable and compelling in Lawson's short stories.

# CONTEXT & BACKGROUND

Henry Lawson's stories engage closely with many of the prevalent issues of their own time, and were popular with readers for that reason. Some knowledge of the society and ideas of late nineteenth-century Australia makes reading the stories more meaningful and rewarding; brief notes about this period are included below. Lawson also drew on his own experiences for material for his fiction, and we first consider some of the intersections between Lawson's life and his preoccupations as a writer.

## Biographical Details

Henry Lawson was born in 1867 at Grenfell, on the NSW goldfields. His father, Niels Larsen, was a Norwegian sailor who settled in Australia during the gold rushes, and registered his name as Lawson.[1]1 For most of Lawson's childhood his parents lived on a selection at New Pipeclay, near Mudgee in central NSW. His story 'A Child in the Dark, and a Foreign Father' is at least partly based on the family's circumstances during these years. Many other stories, including the Joe Wilson sequence, are set in the country around Mudgee and Gulgong.

## Early Successes

In 1883 Lawson's parents separated; his mother, Louisa, moved to Sydney and Henry soon joined her. Louisa Lawson became a prominent publisher and writer. Through his mother, Henry gained familiarity with the radical ideas and political movements of the day, including feminism and republicanism. Louisa encouraged her son's early attempts at writing and published his first collection of stories.

Lawson initially worked as a coach-painter but soon began publishing poems and stories, especially with the *Bulletin* magazine. In the 1890s

---

1 Alternatively, John Barnes claims that Lawson's mother 'changed the family name when registering her son's birth in 1867' (See Barnes's 'Introduction' to *The Penguin Henry Lawson*, pp.5-6).

Lawson worked as a journalist, travelling to Western Australia, Brisbane and later New Zealand. He established his reputation as a poet, but his attention increasingly turned towards the particular demands and possibilities of the short story.

The concerns of Lawson's writing reflect his childhood experiences of the bush as well as social and political ideas promoted by the *Bulletin*, such as Australian nationalism and the fascinations of life in the bush and the outback. The editor of the *Bulletin*, J. F. Archibald, encouraged and partly funded Lawson's trip to Bourke and throughout northwest New South Wales in the summer of 1892-93. This provided Lawson with his only experience of the outback, which he found to be harsh and desolate. Lawson's journalist's eye for detail enabled him to transform the characters and incidents he observed into finely crafted stories such as 'The Union Buries Its Dead' and 'On the Edge of a Plain'.

## Marriage

Lawson's most successful period was from 1896 to 1902. In 1896 the famous collection of stories *While the Billy Boils* was published, including 'The Drover's Wife' and 'The Union Buries Its Dead'. Also in this year, Lawson married Bertha Bredt, whom he had met in the previous year.

Some idea of the qualities of the marriage may be drawn from the Joe Wilson stories. In 1916 Lawson said that: 'Mrs Joe Wilson was ... a portrait of Mrs Henry Lawson (as I idealized her then)'.[2] Bertha Lawson's background was German, and Joe Wilson observes that 'Mary was German in figure and walk' (in 'Water Them Geraniums', p.146). However, unlike the Wilsons, Henry and Bertha never took up a selection — in this, the characters' lives mirror those of Lawson's parents.

Lawson's own personality is reflected in his character, Joe Wilson. In 'Joe Wilson's Courtship', Joe thinks he was 'born a poet by mistake' (p.168), and his fondness for alcohol is introduced apologetically: 'I only drank because I felt less sensitive, and the world seemed a lot saner and better and kinder when I had a few drinks' (p.170). Later, Joe's

**2** Cited in the entry 'Wilson, Joe' in Wilde et al (eds.), *The Oxford Companion to Australian Literature*, Oxford University Press, Melbourne, 1991, p.751.

drinking is a contentious point between the married couple in 'Water Them Geraniums', just as Lawson's alcoholism led to problems in his own marriage.

In 1900, Henry, Bertha and their two children travelled to London, searching for a wider audience for Lawson's writing. At first the trip was successful: the collection *Joe Wilson and His Mates*, including the Joe Wilson quartet and 'The Loaded Dog', was published in London in 1901. By the following year, though, the marriage was failing and the family returned to Sydney.

## Lawson's Decline

In the last twenty years of his life, Lawson wrote little of lasting significance. He separated from his wife and children in 1902, and in subsequent years was imprisoned on several occasions for failing to meet maintenance payments. He suffered from alcoholism and spent time in mental institutions. However, his fame and recognition continued, and when he died in 1922 Lawson was the first Australian writer to be granted a state funeral. His face appeared on the ten-dollar note when decimal currency was introduced in 1966, a sign of his central and lasting importance to Australian culture.

## The *Bulletin* Magazine

Perhaps the most important influence on Lawson's writing career was the *Bulletin* magazine. This weekly magazine was established in 1880 and achieved great success during the 1890s, when its circulation was around 80,000 copies. It promoted new Australian writers of fiction and nonfiction and championed Australian lifestyles and attitudes, as opposed to British models of society and culture. The *Bulletin*, recommending that Australia look after its own interests supported the republican movement of the 1890s (which was, of course, unsuccessful, as it was again at the end of the twentieth century).

The *Bulletin* regarded the bush as the source of key Australian values. This 'bush ethos' entailed such attributes as equality between men (egalitarianism), male mateship, and a stoic fortitude — the ability to endure hardship without much complaint, with the aid of a wry sense of humour and the willingness to help one's fellow man. The *Bulletin* promoted the formation of a national literature, especially in the early 1900s, following Federation. The bush ethos played a central role in the way this literature was envisaged. As well as publishing poems and stories by writers like Lawson, Barbara Baynton and 'Banjo' Paterson, the *Bulletin* published books about bush life such as Steele Rudd's *On Our Selection* (1899) and Joseph Furphy's *Such is Life* (1903), which have become Australian literary classics.

## The *Bulletin*'s Motto: 'Australia for the White Man'

The nationalist agenda advanced by the *Bulletin* was consistent with the White Australia policy adopted by the first Federal government, and was particularly hostile towards Aboriginal and Chinese people. For many years the *Bulletin*'s motto was: 'Australia for the White Man', until in 1960 the magazine's new editor, Donald Horne, removed it.

In Lawson's stories, the expression of anti-Chinese and anti-Aboriginal sentiments can suggest that Lawson himself held these views. Although this may well have been the case, a character's or narrator's opinion is not necessarily that of the author. Chinese characters barely figure in the stories set for study. However, in a later story, 'Ah Soon', the narrator does seem to be Lawson himself, and he makes a quite definite statement:

> I am anti-Chinese as far as Australia is concerned; in fact, I am all for a White Australia. But one may dislike, or even hate, a nation without hating or disliking an individual of that nation.... I never knew or heard of a Chinaman who neglected to pay his debts ... or was not charitable when he had the opportunity.[3]

3 'Ah Soon' is from the sequence 'Elder Man's Lane', published in the *Bulletin* between 1912 and 1920; reprinted in Cecil Mann (ed.), *Henry Lawson's Best Stories*, Angus and Robertson, Sydney, 1966, pp.249-54. See the entry 'Depressions' in Davison *et al* (eds.), *The Oxford Companion to Australian History*, Oxford University Press, South Melbourne, 2001, pp.183-85.

Here, Lawson's opinion of Chinese people includes a certain amount of tolerance, but the overall view of Australian national identity is strongly Anglo-centric.

## Louisa Lawson and the *Dawn*

The *Dawn* was a monthly women's magazine, established and edited by Louisa Lawson; it ran from 1888 to 1905. It was the first Australian feminist magazine, and it employed women whenever possible. The *Dawn* advocated social and political reform in such areas as divorce law and women's suffrage (NSW women obtained the right to vote in 1902). Alongside the *Dawn*'s radical feminist commentaries were more conservative columns about how women could look good and enjoy married life.

Henry Lawson was aware of the feminist movement, and his stories include a number of strong and capable women characters, such as the woman in 'The Drover's Wife', Brighten's sister-in-law, and Mary Wilson and Mrs Spicer in the Joe Wilson sequence. However, these women are not politically active, or even members of the paid workforce, and some critics have criticised Lawson's representations of women as being too limited in their conceptions of women's lives and roles.

## The Depression of the 1890s

In the late 1880s the international price of wool, which was crucial to Australia's economic fortunes, fell dramatically. This followed a period of prosperity witnessed to the undertaking of many major nation-building projects, such as the construction of railways, roads, and irrigation schemes. However, when the wool price dropped, British banks withdrew the money they had placed in Australian banks, leading to a severe economic depression. Historian Jenny Lee notes that: 'In April-May of 1893, 13 of the 16 major banks suspended business'.[4] Lawson alludes to this situation in 'Telling Mrs Baker': the 'world might wobble and all the banks go bung' (p.197). Lawson himself was one of the victims of

4 See the entry 'Depressions' in Davison *et al* (eds), *The Oxford Companion to Australian History*, Oxford University Press, South Melbourne, 2001, pp.183-85.

the depression; he struggled for a time to find work as a journalist in the early 1890s, and he writes about others trying to survive in desperate circumstances from a sympathetic standpoint.

The depression demonstrated how intimately connected Australia's economy was to overseas interests and finances. Some people thought that the solution to this 'problem' was for Australia to become much more isolated from the international economy. These issues are remarkably similar to contemporary anxieties about globalisation and debates about the relative merits of free trade versus tariff protection for national economies. Then, as now, there were many conflicting opinions and no guarantees of economic security.

## Workers and Unions

One of Lawson's prevailing concerns is the struggle for existence of ordinary, working people, and their awareness of social inequities. Some of Lawson's poems forcibly express some of these concerns; 'Faces in the Street', for instance, describes the plight of poor people in cities and imagines an imminent revolution. However, Lawson's stories do not generally advocate radical change in the workplace or to the distribution of wages. In fact, Lawson makes a virtue out of his characters' difficulties, valorising their lack of pretence and material comforts.

The trade union movement had a considerable impact on politics and employer-employee relations in the 1800s, and the number of unions and union memberships increased significantly during this time. But in the 1890s two factors led to a decline in union power. One factor was the depression; the other was the defeat of unions in major disputes. Employers wanted the right to employ non-union labour, while unions wanted to protect the pay and conditions of all employees by unionising workplaces. Governments tended to side with employers, especially when export contracts were at risk. The most significant event was the Maritime Strike in 1890, in which miners and shearers supported the maritime unions. Eventually picket lines were disrupted by special police forces and troops, and the union campaign was defeated in the courts.[5]

5 See 'Maritime Strike' in Davison *et al* (eds.), *The Oxford Companion to Australian History*, p.414.

The decline of the unions during the 1890s is reflected in 'The Union Buries Its Dead', which could be read as a metaphor for the unions assessing their damages after an especially militant period. In the story the union makes possible a funeral for one of its workers in a town in which he is not well known. Although the ceremony brings together members of the local community, the story suggests that ordinary outback people were mostly indifferent to union concerns and politics-and that the unions, in turn, were somewhat remote from the actual lives of the workers.

## Squatters and Selectors

The squatters possessed most of the best farming land in the colonies, and they also held a great deal of political power. Squatting entailed the occupation of vacant Crown land for cattle and sheep grazing. Although initially squatting was illegal, it was effectively legalised when governments imposed an annual licence fee on squatters (from 1837 in NSW).

Many people felt that squatters had unfair access to land. The Selection Acts (passed in 1861 in NSW) were designed to 'open up' land for less affluent farmers, who could purchase their 'selected' land by time-payment. In contrast to the squatters, selectors tended to obtain poorer land and had little money to invest in their land or even to live on. Lawson's stories express approval of the hard-working, egalitarian ethos of the selectors, but are contemptuous of the aristocratic pretensions of the squatters.

## Lawson and 'Banjo' Paterson: the *Bulletin* Debate

Alongside Henry Lawson, the other most famous name from the turn of the twentieth century is A. B. 'Banjo' Paterson, who wrote such well-known ballads as 'The Man from Snowy River', 'Clancy of the Overflow' and 'Waltzing Matilda'. Paterson published poetry about the bush in the *Bulletin*, using the pen name 'The Banjo'. His background was more privileged than Lawson's; he grew up on a station near Yass (in NSW) and later worked as a solicitor in Sydney.

Lawson and Paterson were both influenced by the old bush ballads, but their different approaches fuelled a competitive exchange of poems and articles in the *Bulletin* during the 1890s, known as the '*Bulletin* debate'. Paterson had a romantic view of the bush, and through such characters as 'Saltbush Bill' represented bushmen as folk heroes. Lawson, though, argued for a realistic portrayal of bush or outback life, one which foregrounded its hardships and injustices, its monotony and loneliness.

# GENRE, STYLE & STRUCTURE

## Structure

Most of Lawson's short stories are so simply told that they appear to lack plot or structure. That is, they have no well defined beginning, middle and end, and no real climax or release of tension. Exceptions to this pattern include 'The Loaded Dog' and 'The Drover's Wife'. Also, 'Brighten's Sister-in-Law' begins in a reflective, matter-of-fact tone before suddenly generating a sense of crisis that is finally resolved. In general, though, the narrative tension is maintained at a steady, and not very intense level throughout the stories.

This apparent lack of structure is not a result of Lawson's carelessness in writing; the carefully crafted nature of the stories becomes evident on closer analysis. The evenness of the narrative tone reflects a quality of sameness about bush life and conveys a sense of its inhabitants' steady forbearance. As Lawson observed, there was no great hope for the future and no real relief from daily chores and routines in such an existence; it is this pattern, or lack of it, which strongly informs Lawson's brand of narrative structure.

## Narrative Perspective

Lawson's stories fall into two groups, according to whether the narrative point of view is first-person or third-person. First-person narratives include 'Telling Mrs Baker', 'The Union Buries Its Dead' and the Joe Wilson stories. The narrator is himself a character in these stories, and the way in which the story is told is part of the characterisation of the narrator. Interest is generated by the narrator's attempt to cast himself in a relatively favourable light, or to resolve his predicament.

The yarns told by Jack Mitchell, 'On the Edge of a Plain' and 'Bill, the Ventriloquial Rooster', are also like first-person narratives, although they are framed by a third-person narrator. In the latter story the third-person narrator contributes no more than 'said Mitchell'. Both Mitchell and Joe Wilson are keen observers of others, though Wilson has the more introspective and sentimental personality, while Mitchell possesses the sharper sense of humour.

The other narrative perspective deployed by Lawson is that of a third-person narrator, as in 'The Bush Undertaker', 'The Drover's Wife', 'A Child in the Dark' and 'The Loaded Dog'. Typically, the narrator generates the impression of objectivity, of a spectator faithfully recording events. However, Lawson often varies the attitude (or bias) of the narrator, with respect to the characters and incidents being described, obtaining a range of tones and styles.

For instance, the narrator can position himself — and the narrator is always an implied 'he' — either as superior, or as roughly equal in social status, to the characters. The 'bush undertaker', or Mrs Spicer in 'Water Them Geraniums', are rendered less sophisticated and quick-witted than the narrator since their language is clearly less 'correct'. The old man's expressions in 'The Bush Undertaker' include 'more's unpossible' and 'great an' gerlorious rassaraction' (pp.33, 34); his eccentric behaviour and speech are the source of the story's comedy. This effect depends, in turn, on the narrator and reader taking up a superior, more knowing or 'normal' position from which to 'view' him.

In 'The Drover's Wife', the narrator admires the woman's courage and resourcefulness but occasionally is condescending, as in the phrase: 'Heaven help her! [she] takes a pleasure in the fashion-plates' (p.22). This creates a gap between character and narrator — who, it is implied, not only does not take 'pleasure in the fashion-plates' but regards them as an inferior form of entertainment.

## Style

### Informal and Colloquial

Rather than using an educated, literary tone or 'voice', Lawson typically uses a prose style appropriate to an intelligent observer who is nonetheless part of the moral and social world being described. The stories aim for an appearance of naturalness, as if the narrator is casually telling a yarn rather than painstakingly composing a stylised work of art.

This impression is enhanced by the use of informal or colloquial language, as in Mitchell's description of his rooster Bill: 'a big mongrel of no particular breed' (in 'Bill, the Ventriloquial Rooster', p.73), or 'The Loaded Dog' narrator's assertion that the cartridge 'had been excellently well made' (p.99). Also, expressions like: 'You remember we left little Jim with his aunt' (in 'Water Them Geraniums', p.142) give the impression of familiarity and immediacy, in the manner of an oral narrative.

Perhaps the most sombre tone is that of 'A Child in the Dark, and a Foreign Father', in which the opening, joyful exclamation of 'New Year's Eve!' is immediately succeeded by a description of oppressive heat, drought, and the night's 'smothering darkness' (p.213). The narrative lacks the spontaneous feel of the other stories and uses long, complex sentences such as:

> The road ran along by the foot of a line of low ridges, or spurs, and as he passed the gullies or gaps he felt a breath of hotter air, like blasts from a furnace in the suffocating atmosphere. (p.213)

This prose style is more a written than an oral use of language, and its comprehension requires some thought — the opposite qualities to a 'yarn'.

### Irony and Humour

The dry, laconic humour characteristic of Lawson's narrators often depends on irony for its effect. Sometimes the irony is at the expense of a character, drawing attention to their eccentricity. In 'The Bush Undertaker' the narrator describes the old man's muttering to himself as a 'soliloquy'; the irony here devolves from the technique of exaggeration. A soliloquy is a dramatic speech in which a character with high social status articulates his or her most private thoughts and desires (as in Hamlet's famous soliloquies in Shakespeare's play). In contrast, the old man in 'The Bush Undertaker', who is completely isolated from society, is merely thinking aloud about his dinner.

A different tone is generated in 'The Drover's Wife', in which the woman seems to view the world with the same sense of irony as the narrator. She laughs, for instance, at her attempt to wipe her eyes with a handkerchief full of holes, and she has a 'keen, very keen, sense of the ridiculous' (p.25) that the narrative also seems to approve of and enjoy. This 'sense of the ridiculous' runs through all the stories, with the exception of 'A Child in the Dark, and a Foreign Father'. Humour and laughter allow the characters' sorrows and anxieties to be more lightly borne.

The use of irony enables the stories to maintain a fine balance between the serious and the comic. Many characters find themselves in desperate situations, but Lawson never turns these into tragedy. The stories place the reader in a position of feeling sympathy for the characters, but not of pitying them on the one hand or laughing outright at them on the other. The characters are aware of their circumstances and accept them; they cope as well as possible and make the most of whatever occasions for amusement or contentment come to hand.

# STORY ANALYSES

## 'The Drover's Wife' (pp.19–26)

**Summary:** *A snake disappears under a house near sunset; the woman, whose husband is away droving, sits up throughout the night to protect her children; near dawn, the snake emerges, and the woman kills it.*

First published in the *Bulletin* in 1892, 'The Drover's Wife' remains one of Lawson's most popular and critical successes. Later writers and painters, such as Murray Bail and Russell Drysdale, have taken up its material and reworked it. Barbara Jefferis's story with the same title, published in the *Bulletin* in 1980, comprises a feminist response, and allows the woman herself to narrate the story.

### Narrative Structure

The story follows the course of a single evening after a snake disappears under the house in the late afternoon. The mother — the 'drover's wife' of the title — has sole care of the family; her husband has been away for six months. She maintains a night-long watch for the snake, and her thoughts wander over various aspects of her life: past and present, family and neighbours, experiences of sadness and pleasure. This gives the story its varied texture, a sense not just of a single night passing but of a whole life being lived.

### The Role of the Snake

No description of the snake is given; it is a mysterious threat from without rather than a well-defined quantity. It hides beneath the house, but the barrier between outside and inside is not perfect, since the 'rough slab floor' has cracks in it (p.20). In this way, the snake can be read as being similar to the unconscious — that part of the mind containing fears that ordinarily are suppressed, but that sometimes come to the conscious surface (as in dreams).

To provide some protection against the snake, the woman takes her children into the kitchen, next to the house but with a dirt floor. The basic furnishings and material comforts in the kitchen suggest the qualities of the family's daily struggle for existence. They gather together against a common threat, making do with whatever resources are available. The narrative thus quickly aligns the reader's sympathies with the woman and her children.

### 'There are things that a bushwoman cannot do'

The forces of the natural world seem to be arrayed against this woman: in addition to the snake, there are fires, floods, drought, illness, child-bearing and 'a mad bullock'. There is also the (unstated) sexual threat of single men interested in 'staying for the night' (p.24); figures Lawson calls 'sundowners'. All these threats are greatly increased by the drover's absence. The woman either depends on help from other men — such as the 'four excited bushmen' who help her put out a fire — or fails in her endeavours, as when 'during her husband's absence' a flood destroys their dam (p.23).

### Tears, then Laughter

Although the woman displays resilience and ingenuity in coping with the lonely bush life, she becomes more emotional as the story approaches its climax. Shortly before the snake finally appears in one of the cracks in the partition slabs, 'tears spring to her eyes' as she realises her woodpile has been stacked with a hollow centre by a 'stray blackfellow' (p.25). It is hardly the worst of the many incidents she recalls during the night — which include the death of one of her children — so her tears suggest her increased anxiety and emotional fragility by this time. Then the tears are relieved with a sudden swing to laughter: her handkerchief is so threadbare that her finger and thumb go straight through as she tries to wipe her eyes.

### 'The sickly daylight'

The narrative returns from episodes of the past to the present situation with the phrases 'It must be near one or two o'clock', 'It must be near morning now' and 'It must be near daylight' (pp.22, 25). In this way, the narrative tension is gradually increased. Finally, the snake emerges, and the woman, with the help of the family dog, Alligator, kills it. This releases the tension: the snake burns on the fire and the children go back to sleep. However, the last words of the story, 'the sickly daylight breaks over the bush' (p.26), do not convey a sense of hope or renewal. Instead, the prospect is for a continued struggle for life with few pleasures.

***Q*** What is the effect of the narrative not identifying the woman by her own name?

***Q*** Do you think of the narrator of this story as a man or a woman? Why? (Remember that the narrator is not the same as the author.)

## 'The Bush Undertaker' (pp.27–34)

**Summary:** *A hot Christmas Day; an old man cooks dinner; he digs up some Aboriginal bones, discovers the corpse of his mate Brummy, then buries him.*

The 'bush undertaker' is one of Lawson's most eccentric characters, who is nevertheless depicted sympathetically. This sympathy is generated in part by the harsh conditions in which the old man lives. The loneliness and lack of material comforts he endures might push the most rational person towards eccentricity. Moreover, the action occurs on a Christmas Day, when the man lacks any of the usual trappings of Christmas — family, friends or gifts.

However, the old man manages to sustain and entertain himself by means of his own devising. He talks ceaselessly to himself and his dog Five Bob, and makes as tasty a dinner as his resources allow (a 'doughboy' is a boiled dumpling). He yards the sheep for which he is responsible early enough to make the afternoon a kind of 'holiday', although there is nowhere to go and nothing obvious with which to amuse oneself.

### Aboriginal Bones and White Bones

The old man's fascination with corpses is perhaps a means of coping with two things: the proximity to death inherent in bush life and the absence of others to help deal with it in a dignified fashion. However, the first act the old man performs on his 'holiday' seems, at least to the modern reader, to be very undignified. Neither the character nor the narrator attaches any importance to the removal of the bones of an Aboriginal person from their burial site. The old man handles the bones 'with great care' (p.28) but from a contemporary perspective the unauthorised removal of any bones from their graves demonstrates a *lack* of care or respect. Nor does the narrative suggest what the old man intends to do with the bones; he places them in a bag he seems to have carried with him for that purpose, but does nothing further with them.

In contrast, the old man takes the greatest care to place the remains of Brummy *into* the ground with an improvised, yet reverent, ceremony. The 'undertaker's' serious tone is undercut by the idiosyncratic phrases he uses, such as 'It's time yer turned in, Brum', and 'termorrer's come, Brummy' (p.33). In fact, the affectionate, understated tone of these expressions actually renders the scene quite poignant. The phrase 'in hopes of a great an' gerlorious rassaraction!' (p.34) is at odds with the seemingly hopeless circumstances, a tension that is simultaneously both comic and touching.

### 'The grand Australian bush'

The narrative's emotional content is heightened by expressions such as 'a flood of memories, in which the old man became absorbed' (p.33), and the devotion with which he 'fashioned the mound carefully with his spade' (p.34). Yet the old man, like the narrative itself, refuses to be overcome by sentiment. The last lines revert to the relative detachment of the story's opening: 'the sun sank again on the grand Australian bush' (p.34). The word 'grand' is ironic, since the landscape in this story is anything but grand — rather it is harsh and desolate. Despite a superior tone that renders the old man rather ridiculous, the narrative finally adopts resignation (akin to the old man's resignation to his fate) as the tone with which to bring the story to an appropriate close.

***Q*** How significant is it that the bones dug up by the old man are those of an Aboriginal person, as opposed to a white person?

***Q*** Is the implied reader of this story someone who lives in the bush, or in the city? Do you think Lawson imagined the possibility of an Aboriginal person reading this story?

## 'The Union Buries Its Dead' (pp.40–44)

**Summary:** *A union labourer drowns in the Darling River and is buried in an outback town.*

This is one of Lawson's most compact stories, a seemingly simple description of a funeral that is also a meditation, in some ways world-weary and cynical, on the nature of human life and death. The narrator gives an apparently honest account of what he sees, but the narrative is full of gaps and omissions. The man who dies is introduced as a 'young man on horseback', who is told that the water is 'deep enough to drown him' (p.40). This phrase, of course, anticipates his death, and its grim irony is typical of the narrative tone throughout.

This is the only story set for study that refers to the trade unions. Although the dead man's membership of the General Labourers' Union (the G.L.U.) means that his funeral brings together a small crowd, few people present actually seem to have known him. Nor does the narrator describe the work performed by the union, or reveal the real identity of the dead man. The union is certainly 'burying its dead', but the narrative suggests that the union's concern is quite impersonal, an administrative matter rather than a compassionate act.

### Strangeness and Alienation

In the early part of the narrative, those present are described as 'strangers' to one another, and the repetition of 'strangers' emphasises the characters' lack of connection with each other or to the deceased, generating a sense of alienation. The narrator is drawn into the action as if by chance, and his narrative tone throughout is flat and unemotional. In fact, the lack of emotion becomes the central point of interest. The narrator's indifference to events becomes increasingly marked, as in such expressions as: 'It doesn't matter much — nothing does' and 'we have already forgotten the name' (pp.43, 44).

The narrator observes people acting in strange ways, in particular the 'big, bull-necked publican' who holds the priest's hat above the 'head of his reverence' despite the priest's standing in the shade (p.42). The act is read by the narrator as entirely self-interested, a 'good opportunity' for the man to assert his 'faithfulness and importance to his Church' (p.43). None of the characters, including the cynical narrator, appears capable of a genuinely selfless action or feeling.

### Things Left Unsaid

The narrative leaves many details unstated. The identities of the dead man, and of the narrator, remain unknown. The narrator indicates that the police went to the union office for information, then states: 'That's how we knew' (p.40); yet the connection between these things is unclear. Was the narrator in the union office? Is he a union member? Why does he attend the funeral when he is so indifferent to its progress?

Towards the end of the story, the narrator draws the reader's attention to things omitted from his description:

> I have left out the wattle — because it wasn't there. I have also neglected to mention the heart-broken old mate … he was probably 'Out Back'…. I have left out the 'sad Australian sunset' because the sun was not going down at the time. (p.43)

### Key point

Here, the narrative suggests that romantic, sentimental descriptions of the outback and its inhabitants are inaccurate, and that the reality, which is what ought to be described, is harsh and unsympathetic to human feeling and ceremony. The extreme heat and dryness make the funeral a trial to be endured rather than a deeply felt ritual. These circumstances are exacerbated by its taking place at midday. The sun is directly overhead, as if exposing the townspeople's speeches and actions as empty gestures, the façade rather than the substance of human emotion and spirituality.

***Q*** What is the significance of the union labourer being known by a false name? What is the effect of the narrator's forgetting, and being indifferent to, the true name of this man?

***Q*** How significant is it that the narrator's name and occupation are also unknown?

## 'On the Edge of a Plain' (pp.61–62)

**Summary:** *Mitchell and a mate rest in the shade; Mitchell describes a visit home after an absence of eight years.*

### Mitchell

This story features the character Jack Mitchell, who appears in around forty stories or sketches. Mitchell is at least partly based on J. W. Gordon, with whom Lawson travelled through outback NSW in 1892–93. Lawson also used other people and experiences, including his own, to generate Mitchell's characteristics and repertoire of 'yarns'.

### The 'Yarn'

This genre of story is told in the vernacular; it is informal rather than formal, as if spoken rather than written. All Mitchell's yarns are short, with little or no setting or context for their telling. Instead, Mitchell's narrative quickly places the listener/reader in an altogether different time and place to that in which he tells the story. Like the tall story, the yarn tends to stretch the truth of things for impact and humour. The outlandish aspect of 'On the Edge of a Plain' lies in Mitchell's 'ghostly' arrival the day after his family had been told of his death: 'They thought at first I was a ghost, and then they all tried to get holt of me at once — nearly smothered me' (p.61).

The excessiveness of the family's reaction contrasts with the laid-back tone of Mitchell's narrative, punctuated by mundane comments about the present — 'Look at that pup!' and 'Have you got the knife?' (p.61). The implication is that Mitchell himself was not overcome with emotion, and nor is he particularly sentimental in telling the story.

### Setting

As the title indicates, the two men are 'on the edge of a plain'. The setting merely consists of shade from some mulga trees and the plain onto which the men walk at the end of the story. Their brief rest in the shade is analogous to the brief interlude Mitchell had at home, surrounded by family affection for a week until the demands of work caused him to move on again.

### Key point

Because of this parallel between the content of the yarn and the setting for its narration, the plain takes on a more symbolic meaning. That is, it is like 'life', largely difficult and featureless but containing periodic, brief experiences of rest, human affection and laughter. Thus the sketch-story gestures towards a universal statement, taking outback bushmen as exemplary figures for a rather grim diagnosis of the human condition.

**Q** Why does Lawson keep the description of the plain — 'wide, hot, shadeless' — until the end of the story (rather than, say, placing it at the start)?

**Q** What is the role of Mitchell's dog in this story?

## 'Bill, the Ventriloquial Rooster' (pp.73–77)

**Summary:** *Mitchell tells the story of Bill, a rooster with ventriloquist skills.*

This is another of Mitchell's 'yarns'; Lawson indicated that he based it on events in his own childhood.[6] The narrative is characterised by exaggeration and excess: every incident is remarkable; every moment is filled with interest. There is a naive simplicity to this world of the past — of childhood. Characters fall into well-defined categories, and this is especially so for gender roles. Mitchell's father is 'the old man' and his mother 'the old lady'; their only point of similarity is that they are equally 'stubborn and obstinate' (p.73).

The fight between the roosters, Bill and Jim, is strictly for the men's amusement and is only possible when the women and children are visiting 'some relations, about fifteen miles away' (p.75). Although this marks cockfighting as a strictly male entertainment, the fights themselves are not represented as cruel and vicious. Rather, the animals are active and willing participants who stage a 'grand foight' (p.75).

There is no real malevolence in this world; nor is there much sentiment or kindness. When generosity or thoughtfulness are expressed,

6 John Barnes gives the reference for Lawson's remarks in his notes in *The Penguin Henry Lawson*, p.224.

they take an unfussy, understated form. For instance, the Mitchells' Irish neighbour, Page, acknowledges Bill's victory over his own white rooster with a solemn concession: 'I bear no malice' (p.75); and Jack's presence on the roof is not betrayed by the other men but they 'gave me the office whenever the old man happened around' (p.76).

The story invests life 'on the selection' with a mythical quality, and thus provides a balance to other Lawson stories about selectors, such as 'Water Them Geraniums'. These stories depict a constant struggle for existence, a proximity to death and a familiarity with loneliness and despair. In contrast, 'Bill, the Ventriloquial Rooster' describes the men's determination to gather together, providing each other with company and entertainment.

### Blending Human and Animal Qualities

In the manner of myths and fairytales, Mitchell represents the animals as having human qualities. This is particularly so for Bill who is a ventriloquist, albeit an unwitting one. Bill's anxious listening and searching 'all over the place for that other rooster' (p.74), and his eagerness to challenge the other rooster to a fight, give him the personality of an earnest country boy who is somewhat slow to figure things out.

Complementing the comic personification of farm creatures, the human characters are given animal-like attributes. Mitchell and his brother avoid Page by hiding 'under the house like snakes' (p.75). The intermingling of human and animal worlds is reinforced when the 'father of a hiding' Bill receives from Page's 'game-rooster' is mimicked by the 'stepfather of a hiding' Mitchell receives from his father (p.77).

### Breaking the Monotony of Existence

What is most desired in this world is relief from day-to-day tedium. Even the roosters seek to vary the pattern of their chase: 'now and then they'd go over the top to break the monotony' (p.77). This could be a metaphor for the lives of the selectors, for their need, now and then, to do something 'over the top' in order to interrupt the sameness of bush life. Perhaps, too, this is a metaphor for Mitchell's storytelling, which is often 'over the top' in its exaggeration of ordinary people and events, enlivening them with humour and drama and adding the occasional note of pathos — such as Bill's sudden death at the story's end. Even here, the sentimental is spliced with the comic, since Bill dies not from exhaustion or injury but from self-disgust, an utterly human and un-rooster-like quality.

***Q*** Explain what is really meant by the phrase: 'a thorough-bred bull ... got into our paddock on account of me mending a panel in the party fence, and carelessly leaving the top rail down after sundown' (p.75).

## 'The Loaded Dog' (pp.94–100)

**Summary:** *Andy, Dave and Jim are mining for gold; Andy makes a cartridge that their dog, Tommy, drags through the campfire, lighting the fuse; the three men flee, chased by Tommy; the cartridge explodes outside the local pub, killing a vicious cattle-dog and causing much hilarity.*

'The Loaded Dog' is Lawson's most famous story and perhaps the best-known story in Australian literature. It is one of several stories featuring Dave Regan, Andy Page and Jim Bently; Dave Regan is even referred to near the end of 'A Double Buggy at Lahey's Creek', sending the Wilsons the gift of a fresh-water cod.

The narrative voice is wryly amused by the events described, slightly more knowing than Dave, Jim and Andy but respectful of their resourcefulness and know-how. A note of irony is introduced immediately:

> Dave Regan, Jim Bently, and Andy Page were sinking a shaft at Stony Creek in search of a rich gold quartz reef which was supposed to exist in the vicinity. There is always a rich reef supposed to exist in the vicinity.... (p.94)

The word 'supposed' conveys the narrator's scepticism about the existence of such a 'rich reef'. This tone continues through the opening paragraph, concluding with the 'usual' (but undesired) result: 'an ugly pot-hole ... and half a barrow-load of broken rock' (p.94).

The contrast between the men's earnest commitment and the sceptical tone of the narrator prompts the reader's expectation that things will not proceed according to plan. Once the cartridge, a 'formidable bomb', is complete, the narrative introduces the dog Tommy, a 'big, foolish, four-footed mate' (p.96). The juxtaposition of these two things sets the scene for the farce that unfolds once Tommy picks up the cartridge and drags the fuse through the fire.

The narrative pace increases and the dog's playful, human (albeit childlike) qualities come to the fore: it 'whooped joyously' and 'grinned sardonically' (p.98). The narrative tracks the dog's wild chase, following the three men in turn. The ending is delayed by one device after another; as well as describing the men's strategies for escape, the narrative draws the reader's attention to peripheral details such as Andy's recollection of a 'picture of the Russo-Turkish war with a circle of Turks lying flat on their faces' (p.98). Andy's memory is irrelevant to the plot, but it adds to the overall colour and style of the narrative, as well as deferring its climax.

Dave runs to the local hotel, which is promptly vacated when Tommy enters by the back door. A 'happy' ending is assured when a 'vicious yellow mongrel cattle dog' chases Tommy away and, at the pivotal moment, sniffs at the cartridge (p.99). The narrative pauses over an account of the cattle dog's disagreeable 'personality', followed by a list of the types of dogs that converge on the yard. Finally, the inevitable, climactic explosion causes the remains of the cattle dog to be left 'lying against the paling fence' (p.99), while the other dogs, maimed and scarred, take flight. No one is injured and there is no significant damage to property, ensuring that the story's comic tone and genre are sustained right to the end.

The men and women at the hotel find the episode hilarious, and it takes on mythical proportions in subsequent years. The narrative draws back from that moment in time, to look across the 'years afterwards' (p.100), suggesting that such extraordinary, fabulous incidents belong to the frontier past rather than the settled present. The story's ending thus acquires an element of nostalgia, marking a shift from the sceptical tone of the opening and generating a satisfied sense of closure.

***Q*** Would this story be as effective if narrated in first-person — say, by Dave Regan?

## The Joe Wilson Quartet: an Overview

The Joe Wilson quartet comprises four extended stories: 'Joe Wilson's Courtship', 'Brighten's Sister-in-Law', 'Water Them Geraniums' and 'A Double Buggy at Lahey's Creek'. Lawson also wrote six other stories about Joe Wilson, mostly with Joe as the narrator. The first story in the quartet is the only one not set for study, but it is nevertheless worth reading as background for the other three. It tells the story of Joe's meeting and courtship of Mary Brand, and it is infused with sentiment and nostalgia, as well as hints of the less happy times that followed.

Considered collectively, the Joe Wilson quartet is the nearest thing to a novel that Lawson wrote. The four stories are strongly linked by narrative voice, character, setting and incident. The mood of 'Joe Wilson's Courtship' is of fond recollection; 'Brighten's Sister-in-Law' and 'Water Them Geraniums' are darker in tone, punctuated by quarrels between Joe and Mary, encounters with death and experiences of hardship. Then, in 'A Double Buggy at Lahey's Creek', Joe and Mary recover something of the tenderness of their courtship, thus recalling the first story in the sequence and generating a sense of closure similar to that expected in a novel.

### A Fluid Sense of Time

Lawson's approach to time in the quartet is fluid, reflecting the temporal jumps of memory as Joe recollects incidents and emotions. For instance, the second story, 'Water Them Geraniums', begins with the Wilsons moving to their Lahey's Creek selection, prior to the main episode in 'Brighten's Sister-in-Law'. Similarly, in 'A Double Buggy at Lahey's Creek', the last of the quartet, Joe begins by referring to incidents in the earliest days of his marriage. The narratives tend to be episodic and disjointed, rather than resembling continuous threads, although each story proceeds chronologically.

### Key point

Joe's thoughts do not only pertain to the particular time being described, but range across all the intervening time covered by memory: 'the hard days went on, and the weeks, and the months, and the years — Ah, well!' ('Brighten's Sister-in-Law', p.110). The narrative thus places individual circumstances and feelings within the context of the Wilsons' entire lives, giving an 'epic' feel to the overall sequence, quite different to the limited time frame of a conventional story.

## 'Brighten's Sister-in-Law' (pp.103–122)

**Summary:** *Joe Wilson brings his three-year-old son, Jim, from Gulgong to the selection at Lahey's Creek; that evening, Jim becomes ill, and Joe rides to the Brightens for help; Brighten's sister-in-law saves Jim.*

The story opens with the birth of Joe and Mary's first child, Jim, when they are living in Gulgong. Jim's teething problems are introduced immediately, and the word 'lance' occurs four times in the fourth paragraph in association with teeth and gums. These images foreground both the vulnerability of flesh and the need for a stoical endurance of life's pains — to be, like Jim, 'a plucky little chap' (p.103).

### Narrative pace

Matter-of-fact expressions like 'Jim was born on Gulgong' and 'Mary and I had been married about two years' (p.103) give little hint of the tense circumstances at the centre of the story. Joe indicates that Jim's 'first turn ... was the worst' (p.104), suggesting that subsequent episodes were relatively harmless and keeping the reader's sense of expectation low.

Joe reflects on how children should be raised, on 'old-fashioned children' and on his fencing and carrying work; all of which makes the narrative pace slow and meditative. This renders the subsequent turn of events all the more dramatic. It also establishes Joe's reflective personality, and Mary's objections to this personality trait; she asks: 'What's the use of always worrying and brooding?' (p.110), a question Joe himself is never able to answer.

### The Tension Increases

Joe takes Jim from Gulgong to Lahey's Creek for the first time, and they 'camp out' overnight. Jim does not eat his dinner, and Joe's comments 'it was a bad sign' and 'I was scared now' (pp.113–14) effect a sudden shift in tone. In fact, the tone becomes more melancholic before this, through

Joe's contemplation of the surrounding, 'dreary' and 'gnarled' country, and the sound of the creek oaks, 'sigh-sigh-sighing' (p.111). Joe notices Jim looking 'as if he'd been a child for a hundred years or so' (p.112). This echoes the earlier description of Jim's appearance immediately prior to illness as 'old-fashioned' (p.105), and thus anticipates the new threat to Jim's life.

Jim becomes feverish, and Joe appeals to God. He sees 'the figure of a woman, all white' descending through the trees and pointing 'up the road' (p.114). This image transforms the matter-of-fact narrative into one with supernatural or gothic qualities. Joe describes the bush as ghostly and haunted by spirits — a kind of equivalent to the haunted house of a traditional gothic story. The trees have 'ghostly blue-white bark' and the bush seems 'full of ghosts' (p.116). Joe and Jim ride through 'Dead Man's Hollow' and finally see the house 'at the back of a ghostly clearing' (p.117). Death is personified, as in the expression 'if death came along' (p.114) and the figure of the 'strange horse' that Joe 'feels' is riding immediately behind (p.116).

Jim has a fit just as they arrive at the Brightens', and Joe feels that events are beyond his control: 'I even thought of Mary and the funeral' (p.117). Then the 'sister-in-law' provides the necessary treatment, and Jim is 'back for the world again' (p.118).

### Brighten's Sister-in-Law

Joe is fascinated by the woman's commanding presence and expertise amidst such ordinary surroundings and company. Her sister, Mrs Brighten, is a 'washed-out, helpless little fool of a woman', while Brighten is 'a nuggety little hairy man' (p.118). It is as if they belong to a bush underclass, shrunken and inferior. In contrast, Joe perceives Brighten's sister-in-law to be almost larger than life: 'a big woman, her hands and feet were big, but well-shaped and all in proportion' (p.119). Joe surreptitiously watches her, and observes that 'two great tears dropped from her wide open eyes ... in the firelight they seemed tinged with blood' (p.120). There is a sense of mystery about the woman's past; Joe sees her 'haggard and hopeless' look (p.120), the reasons behind which are never explained.

The woman keeps her feelings under tight control, and she firmly instructs the others how to behave: she tells Joe to 'go to bed', and her sister to put away 'the black bottle' (p.120). In melodramatic contrast, Joe goes out to his horse and, with his 'arms round her neck ... cried for the second time since I was a boy' (p.120). The horse cries too, in keeping with the strange events of the night.

Jim and Joe remain at the Brightens' for another day and night, providing the story with a tranquil coda. The evening meal is a celebratory occasion of laughter and conversation, elevated by the civilised qualities of Brighten's sister-in-law. Questions about how she became so knowledgeable are implicit in the narrative, but Joe has no means by which to resolve them.

As the Wilsons prepare to leave on the following morning, Joe contemplates his own emotions and those of Jim and Brighten's sister-in-law. Jim's mouth is 'twitching', while Joe's attempt to speak only results in his voice sounding 'like an ungreased wagon-wheel' (p.122). As on the night of Jim's illness, he observes tears in the woman's eyes and, as they drive away, 'that haggard, hungry, hopeless look' (p.122). Once again, the woman's real feelings, and their underlying causes, remain mysterious.

***Q*** What is the significance of Joe not knowing, or not stating, the name of Brighten's sister-in-law?

## 'Water Them Geraniums' (pp.142–167)

**Summary:** *The Wilsons arrive at their selection; their neighbour, Mrs Spicer, is eccentric but faces hardship with dignity and determination.*

### 'A lonely track'

Joe and Mary take their first journey together to their new selection at Lahey's Creek. Joe describes the 'track' along which they travel as a 'dreary, hopeless track' (p.143), suggesting that he is reflecting not so much on the course of the track as on the course of his own life. The track is perceived to be 'lonely' because, although Mary and Joe drive along it together, they have grown apart emotionally: 'what strangers we were to each other', Joe realises (p.145). The track's apparent aimlessness might also apply to Lawson's narrative technique, since there is no strong sense of plot or narrative tension.

The landscape's 'lonely, changeless miles' (p.144) suggest the qualities of the Wilsons' lives, steady but without much variety or progress. Joe understands that Mary aspires to 'better things', but he also acknowledges the tendency to 'brood' or 'dream' that sometimes prevents him from accomplishing things. This too is metaphorically represented in terms of travelling: 'I saw a road clear before me, but shied at the first check' (p.144).

### A Tense Arrival

The notes of estrangement and death mark the Wilsons' arrival at their new home, a roughly constructed hut. Joe recalls that the previous selector had left 'because his wife died here' (p.145). Joe and Mary quarrel soon after arriving; Mary resents their remoteness and isolation, and blames Joe's weakness for alcohol as the reason they couldn't move to the city. These frustrations and resentments never entirely recede, but to a certain extent they mark this moment, about halfway through the quartet, as a low point in the Wilsons' lives within the overall sequence.

Joe walks along the creek, and the narrative flashes forward to a time when Mary is lying 'white and still' (p.148), perhaps dead or dying, before returning to the evening being described. Joe despairs 'Why did I bring her here?' (p.148), then hears his neighbour, whom he remembers as a 'gaunt, haggard Bushwoman', calling out to her children (p.149). She represents a warning to Joe 'like a whipstroke on my heart — that this was what Mary would come to if I left her here' (p.150). Joe decides to encourage Mary to leave, but when he returns to their hut Mary has begun to make it more homely. He grudgingly accepts her assurance that 'We'll soon get things shipshape' (p.150).

### The Story's Title

Mrs Spicer calls to her daughter, Annie, to 'water them geraniums!', introducing the phrase that gives the story its title; Joe recalls the 'few dirty grey-green leaves' near the house (p.149). These flowers — the chooks 'scratch dust over them' and ashes are tossed on them — suggests the difficulty of achieving anything more than mere survival in these circumstances. Yet the geraniums are also a metaphor for Mrs Spicer's tenacity, of her capacity to survive despite the challenges dealt to her in life.

The incorrect grammar of the expression — as opposed to 'water *those* geraniums' — suggests Mrs Spicer lacks a formal education, in keeping with Joe's presumption that she has neither 'the brains or the memory' to know or imagine a larger world than the one she inhabits (p.149). However, as Joe comes to know Mrs Spicer better, he becomes increasingly sympathetic and respectful towards her.

### 'Past Carin''

The second section of the story develops the character of Mrs Spicer. She claims to be 'past carin'', but on one level the words are ironic since her actions show her to be genuinely caring. Even her very last words are about the duty of care — instructions to Annie 'to feed the pigs and calves; and ... be sure to water them geraniums' (p.167). Alternatively, the words 'past carin'' could be read as literally true, as indicative of the mindlessly repetitive nature of Mrs Spicer's existence and her mechanical performance of chores and routines.

Joe describes the 'loneliness and dullness' of the Australian bush and the danger that its inhabitants may go mad (p.151). He attributes Mary's ability to cope to the occasional company of travellers, and her determination to remain 'civilised'. The intention to retain the trappings of town life in the bush appears slightly eccentric, but Joe realises that it constitutes a strategy for surviving not just physically but mentally, in a place where social interactions occur infrequently.

The narrative devolves into a series of anecdotes about Mrs Spicer and her family. Its episodes, and the character of Mrs Spicer herself, bear out Joe's anxieties about the bush making its inhabitants 'do queer things, and think queer thoughts' (p.151).

### Mrs Spicer and her Family

On the Wilsons' first morning on the selection, Tommy Spicer visits and brings a generous 'piece of beef ... fresh and clean' (p.152). Mary at first interprets this not as a gift but as an item available for purchase, but Tommy indignantly replies: 'We ain't that sorter people, missus' (p.153). The incident conveys the spirit of bush generosity, and begins to correct Joe's initial impression of the Spicers as rather incompetent and ignorant.

Joe's description of the Spicers' home emphasises its primitive construction, its lack of comfort or decoration. The Spicers survive by trading the butter and eggs they produce for 'flour, tea and sugar' (p.156). Most of the farm work seems to be done by Mrs Spicer, whom Joe observes undertaking physically demanding tasks in the most adverse conditions, such as 'humping great buckets of sour milk to the pigs' in the summer heat (p.158).

### Encounters with Death

The narrative tone becomes more serious when Mrs Spicer describes two encounters with death. The first is of a squatter 'who used to go wrong in his head every now and again, and try to commit suicide' (p.163). Fascinatingly, Lawson leaves unresolved the question of whether this man did or did not survive the incident in which his men chose, as Mrs Spicer says, to 'let him hang for a while' (pp.163–64). The second encounter with death concerns a man 'in the horrors of drink' (p.164), who had visited the Spicers requesting a drink and later hanged himself nearby. The children had been appalled by the sight of the man hanging from a tree by his two saddle straps, though Mrs Spicer claims to have 'got past carin' for anythink now' (p.165).

Mrs Spicer's eldest son at home, Billy, is arrested for stealing a horse from the neighbouring squatter, Wall. Joe unsuccessfully attempts to reason with Wall, but then the squatter's son (also named Billy) intervenes, and the charge is withdrawn. However, Joe observes that 'poor Mrs Spicer was never the same after that' (p.166). Finally, Mrs Spicer's death generates a sense of closure, even though the narrative lacks an obvious structure. Annie relates to the Wilsons her mother's final words, 'be sure and water them geraniums'; Joe wryly comments that, at last, Mrs Spicer is "past carin" right enough' (p.167). The repetition of Mrs Spicer's characteristic expressions gives them added weight and pathos, generating a wistful note with which to conclude the story.

***Q*** How does the absence of other Bushwomen with whom Mrs Spicer might be compared affect your opinion of her?

## 'A Double Buggy at Lahey's Creek' (pp.123–141)

**Summary:** *Mary desires a buggy; Joe describes their difficulties, then their luck, including a successful crop of potatoes; he secretly purchases a double buggy then surprises Mary with it.*

This story charts the gradual improvements in the Wilsons' lives. Joe recalls a series of misfortunes from the early years of the marriage, with Mary's continually thwarted desire for a buggy being the common thread. On one occasion Joe cut his foot 'and was laid up'; later he 'built a woolshed and didn't get paid for it' (p.123). Mary was ill when Jim was born, and the extra expenses meant 'the buggy idea was knocked on the head' (p.124). Joe made a couple of spring-carts, and the possibility of acquiring a buggy does not recur 'until after we'd been settled at Lahey's Creek for a couple of years' (p.124) — which brings the narrative up to the time of the end of 'Water Them Geraniums'.

### Mary's Obstinacy

The main event in this first section, 'Spuds, and a woman's obstinacy', is the Wilsons' successful potato crop. The seed potatoes are sown at Mary's insistence and despite Joe's opposition: 'Mary was obstinate when she got an idea into her head' (p.126), he says. This remark reveals Joe's own shortcomings as much as Mary's, since he is clearly at least as obstinate as Mary and quick to criticise her. Mary's initiative and persistence pay off when good rains lead to 'the finest crop of potatoes ever seen in the district' (p.128).

### Joe's Luck

If the success of the potato crop is mostly due to Mary, the story's second section suggests that the Wilsons' improving fortunes are, on the whole, a result of Joe's hard work and good judgement. Mary again raises the idea of the buggy, but instead their money is used to purchase a flock of sheep from a drought-affected property. The Wilsons have 'luck' in the sense that they receive good rains, but prudent spending is the real key to their success. They expand their property and stock, but Joe still resists buying a buggy, which leads to another argument — 'about the worst quarrel we had' (p.130).

Joe reflects on the paradox of his parsimonious attitude: 'I used to be happier when I was mostly hard up — and more generous' (p.131). Then he thinks about Mary's isolation and her inability to travel around with the two young children, and his thoughts about the buggy begin to shift.

#### Mary's 'Sacrifice'

Joe inspects a new double buggy made by the Galletly brothers, and he considers whether or not to buy it. This marks a transition stage, between the previous times when Joe felt money was better spent on other things, and the next section in which buying the buggy seems the best idea of all. Joe has a glimpse of an alternative life for Mary, in which she might have married a squatter and been 'mistress of Haviland homestead, with servants to wait on her' (p.134).

Instead, the reality is that Mary is 'out there in the lonely hut on a barren creek in the Bush' (p.135). Thus Mary's 'sacrifice' is her choice of a life of hardship with Joe in preference to a life of comfort with an affluent squatter. Joe now appreciates Mary's devotion more than ever, and he decides to purchase the buggy.

#### 'The Buggy Comes Home'

Joe resolves to conceal the buggy's purchase from Mary until her brother, James, can bring it back to Lahey's Creek. The inevitable ending is deferred by narrative asides, such as the conversation between Joe and James (pp.136–37). Joe cajoles James into collecting the buggy; James bargains for a double-barrel gun. Then Joe keeps the buggy a secret from Mary for the three days it takes for James to return.

On the third evening, Joe teases Mary about a buggy and Mary complains about Joe's 'worrying and brooding and making both our lives miserable' (p.138). They are on the verge of arguing until Mary relates an earlier incident, in which Jim had sworn at his go-cart; they laugh and the tension between them eases. The buggy finally arrives, full of gifts from various acquaintances.

### Key point

The buggy is a sign of Mary and Joe's material achievements, and helps to restore the affection between them. After trying out the seat of the buggy, they climb down and sit 'side by side, on the edge of the verandah, and talked more than we'd done for years' (p.141). Their mutual feeling 'just like ... the day we were married', as Mary puts it, brings to a close the sequence of four stories, marked by hardship, anger, anxiety and disappointment, on a positive, if sentimental, note.

***Q*** Do Joe's comments about the well-off Blacks suggest that he is envious of them? Or does Joe accept his place in the social order?

***Q*** Joe thinks of Mary 'doing the work of a station manager as well as that of a housewife and mother' (p.135) — what does this imply about what Joe thinks Mary's work ought to be? Does the narrative indicate what Mary thinks about her work duties?

## 'Telling Mrs Baker' (pp.196–209)

**Summary:** *Two drovers, Jack and Andy, are hired for a long trip; their boss, Bob Baker, is a mate of Andy's, but turns out to be a womaniser and a drunk; Jack and Andy stick by him; he dies, and his mates decide to tell a more flattering story to his wife.*

### Two Halves

This story is in two halves, of which the second is the 'telling' referred to in the title. The first section describes the droving trip undertaken by the narrator, Jack, his mate Andy and their boss, Bob Baker. Bob drinks excessively and has an affair with a barmaid, making it impossible to keep the cattle moving along the stock routes; consequently, he is sacked. Jack and Andy choose to remain with Bob, trying to restrain and care for him. Jack explains their loyalty by stating: 'it isn't Bush religion to desert a mate in a hole; and the Boss was a mate of ours' (p.198). Despite the help of his mates, Bob runs out of money, gets into fights, tries to hang himself and then dies 'in the horrors' (p.199). Bob's brother, Ned, arranges the funeral, and Jack and Andy return south.

In the second section, Jack and Andy 'tell Mrs Baker' about her husband's death. Andy falsifies the actual events in order to spare Mrs Baker the hurt of her husband's betrayal, telling her instead that Bob had died of 'the fever'. Mrs Baker is extremely distraught, and believes the sentimental story fabricated by Andy. However, her educated, literary sister from the city, Miss Standish, is more sceptical.

As a foil to Mrs Baker's distress, the narrative acquires a comic note in this section due to Jack's infatuation with Miss Standish: 'the prettiest girl I'd ever seen' (p.205). Humour also derives from the men's discomfort in this situation, having to lie to the women and survive Miss Standish's penetrating glances. Finally, Andy tells Miss Standish most of the truth, and she expresses her gratitude and admiration for the men as they leave, giving them each a parting kiss 'fair and square on the mouth' (p.209).

### Narrative Voice and Moral Judgements

Although Jack is a participant in these events, he is more of an observer than an initiator of action. He is not, however, an unbiased narrator, but takes a moralistic stance with regard to the various characters. He establishes Bob Baker's weak character from the start, suggesting that that Bob had spent money too freely when he had been a well-off squatter. However, Jack also attributes some of the blame for Bob Baker's demise to the publican who employed barmaids 'as baits for chequemen' (p.197). Bob is thus represented both as culpable and as a victim of circumstances.

When Ned fights the publican and gives him 'nearly as good a thrashing as he deserved', Jack's unqualified approval is evident (p.199). The local police look on without intervening, thus also sanctioning Ned's actions. The implication is that Ned, Jack, Andy and the police are on the side of justice, and that the publican, despite not having broken the law, is in the wrong.

Jack asserts his moral convictions throughout the narrative, but ultimately he depends greatly on Andy for guidance. Despite the steadfast friendship between the two men, Jack emerges as a rather isolated and wistful figure. He lacks a family or a wife of his own, and despite his yearnings has no prospects of forming a relationship with Miss Standish, admitting that: 'she was far and away above me, and the case was hopeless' (pp.205–6).

***Q*** Is Miss Standish's assertion that 'the Bushmen' are 'grand men — they are noble' (p.208) borne out by the actions of Andy and Jack? Or does she romanticise them, thus illustrating the remoteness of city people from the actual lives of bush people?

***Q*** What role does the painting of Wellington at Waterloo, hanging on the Bakers' wall, play in the story?

## 'A Child in the Dark, and a Foreign Father' (pp.213–219)

**Summary:** *On a New Year's Eve, Nils comes home and finds the house dirty and untidy, his wife Emma in bed and his eldest son unwell; he tries to restore order and provide comfort but receives little gratitude; he returns to work early the next morning.*

This story provides an interesting hint about the marriage between Lawson's parents. Like the central character in the story, Lawson's father was also a 'foreign father'; the house's location, near 'the crossing at Pipeclay Creek' (p.213), is reminiscent of the Lawsons' selection at New Pipeclay. The narrative's sympathies lie with the father, who is contemptuous of his wife's writing efforts, while the mother is demanding and self-indulgent. However, it is important to remember that this is not a strictly autobiographical narrative, but is constructed like a conventional story, and is best analysed as fiction rather than fact.

### Narrative Perspective

The father provides the story with its central point of view. At first the narrative adopts an omniscient viewpoint, sketching the 'scrub-covered ridges' then focussing on the road, the fence and the house's exterior — 'whitewashed slab walls and a bark roof' — before moving inside (p.213). The point of view then becomes more personal, following the man's gaze around the kitchen. His calm observation of this scene of domestic neglect changes suddenly with his discovery of a book containing 'verse, in a woman's hand', that he unsuccessfully attempts to tear (p.214). The narrative thus implies that the woman has found time to write poetry, but not to clean the house, while the man has been working in the oppressive summer heat. The narrative's allegiance to the man, rather than the woman, is thus sharply drawn.

Despite the man's anger, he remains calm and tender towards his family, including his wife. He finds his eldest son unwell and restlessly trying to sleep on the living room floor; a younger son is asleep in the next room. This room is partially scrubbed, just as the attempts to cook dinner and wash up remain unfinished. In the main bedroom the man's wife is sleeping, with the remains of her meal left on the chest of drawers. The tense relationship between husband and wife is established by the short conversation between them when she wakes. Emma has only complaints and accusations for her husband, Nils, while he tries to answer patiently.

That the difficulties in the marriage are more the fault of the woman than the man is indicated by the contradictions between what she says and what the narrative describes as being the case. For instance, her claim to have been 'calling for the last half-hour' is inconsistent with the narrative's evidence that she had been 'fast asleep' (pp.215–16). Her reference to herself as 'your clever wife' seems vain, and the fact that the house appears a 'wretched hole' (p.217) is clearly as much her responsibility as her husband's.

### Growing up to be a Man

The man returns to his son, who is increasingly unwell, and recalls 'convulsions amongst the children while they were teething' (p.218). This in turn recalls Joe Wilson's experiences with Jim in 'Brighten's Sister-in-Law'. Another link with this Joe Wilson story is the boy's question: 'it'll be a good while yet before I grow up to be a man, won't it, father?' (p.218). In the earlier story, Jim Wilson asks his father: 'do you think I'll ever grow up to be a man?', which makes Joe remember his own 'childish dread of growing up to be a man' (p.112). In 'A Child in the Dark', though, the father reassures his son, suggesting that worrying about becoming a man will only make it happen 'all the sooner' (p.219).

The tense relationship between husband and wife contrasts with the closeness of the bond between father and son. They lie side by side and hand in hand 'as was customary with them', and eventually the boy falls asleep (p.219). The 'old year died' and the man rises at four the following morning. His long hours of hard, physical work include 'his trade', apparently the family's main source of income, as well as his attempt to 'make a farm and a home' (p.219).

The unremarkable way in which this New Year's Eve passes reflects the tedious, unvarying nature of the family's existence. In this context, the woman's desire to write and read can be understood as a reaction to an existence so limited in its material and emotional possibilities. However, the narrative resists treating her sympathetically. She wakes much later in the morning, begins complaining almost at once and demands to be brought 'a cup of tea and the *Australian Journal*' (p.219).

## Key point

At the end of the story, the narrative point of view switches from the father to the boy. In the father's absence, the boy performs chores around the house and farm and responds to his mother's demands. The boy's anxieties about having to take up adult responsibilities very early in life are thus shown to be well-founded.

***Q*** What is the significance of Nils being unable to tear Emma's exercise book at his 'first savage tug' (p.214)?

***Q*** Does the narrative suggest that Emma is indeed 'misunderstood', as the word written in the exercise book suggests? Or does it suggest that it is actually Nils who is misunderstood by his wife?

# CHARACTERS & RELATIONSHIPS

## Men

**Key quotes**

'I like the Bushmen! They are grand men — they are noble' ('Telling Mrs Baker', p.208)

'What women some men are!' ('Water Them Geraniums', p.148)

'The mate guffawed and Mitchell grinned' ('On the Edge of a Plain', p.62)

Throughout Lawson's stories, certain qualities and values of masculinity recur, and pertain to men who spend almost all of their lives in the bush. Such men are physically able; possess practical know-how; are modest and self-effacing; work hard and enjoy a drink when the opportunity and/or money is available. Too much fondness for alcohol, though, is represented as being a genuine threat to one's physical and emotional wellbeing, a threat that these male characters must continually ward off; but occasionally they succumb.

Lawson's male characters have a sense of humour to which an appreciation of life's ironies and incongruities is central. For instance, in 'The Union Buries Its Dead' someone calls out 'There's the Devil' when the priest comes into view (p.42). Similarly, Mitchell delights at things turning out in the opposite manner to what is expected, such as his family's initially thinking him a ghost rather than welcoming him home (in 'On the Edge of a Plain'). Even Andy's false story about Bob Baker's death includes a few jokes of this nature, such as his characterisation of the publican as an extremely kind man who 'wouldn't take a penny' ('Telling Mrs Baker', p.206) — a complete reversal of the man's true personality.

### Men's Work

The willingness and ability to take on hard, manual work is common to all the central male characters. Joe Wilson anticipates that his brother-in-law, Jim, will 'find enough work at Lahey's Creek to keep him out of mischief' ('Brighten's Sister-in-Law', p.108), implying that a lack of work leads to poor behaviour. Likewise, Mitchell's family encourages him to move on 'because I couldn't get any work to do' ('On the Edge of a Plain', p.62), despite his having been home for only a week after an eight-year absence.

Joe Wilson places a value on hard work in relation to his tendency to drink excessively, asserting that: 'I could keep well away from it so long as I worked hard in the bush' ('Water Them Geraniums', pp.147–48). Working hard, in this formulation, is not only the means to survive but also a moral force. The old man in 'The Bush Undertaker' laments that his mate Brummy could 'earn mor'n any man in the colony, but yer'd lush it all away' (p.29). The tension between drink and work is clear; work is good and leads to profit and success, while drink leads to loss. The male characters who have a virtually endless capacity for work and little desire for drink (or other forms of pleasure) are particularly esteemed in Lawson's stories.

### Jack Mitchell — the itinerant bushman

Jack Mitchell is an archetypal, itinerant bushman, travelling widely and taking on manual work when and where he finds it. He is of slightly quicker intelligence than most of his colleagues, and a keen observer of men's habits and weaknesses. This helps make him an expert storyteller, and his role in these stories is chiefly as a narrator. His narratives are infused with his own character, with his sense of irony and his distinctive, laconic style.

Mitchell's inventiveness is evident in his creative responses to awkward situations. In 'Bill, the Ventriloquial Rooster', Mitchell is determined to see the cockfight, but his father insists that he accompanies his mother 'on a visit to some relations' (p.75). Mitchell pretends that his pony 'went lame' (p.76) and then hides for several hours on the roof of the shed to escape his father's notice. As such, he demonstrates the resourcefulness and tenacity that lie at the heart of the mythology of the bushman, qualities present here in the guise of childhood play that will later be harnessed in the adult world of work.

### Joe Wilson — the versatile, resourceful bushman

On one level Joe Wilson is a typically resourceful bushman who has little affection for the city and can turn his hand and mind to any task required on the land. On another level, though, he displays a propensity for self-examination and sentiment that is rarely evident in Lawson's other bushmen. As an older man, with the benefit of hindsight, Joe regrets his obstinacy as a young man, but also understands the motivations and feelings lying behind his actions. He recalls the time when Mary lay 'white and still' and he had promised to 'give in', but he also understands his determination as a younger man not to comply with Mary's every wish, but rather to 'make a stand' ('Water Them Geraniums', p.148). What links older and younger versions of the character is the brooding tone of the narrative, indicating that Joe's tendency towards 'worrying and brooding' (pp.110, 138) is a lasting and characteristic quality.

A self-important aspect to Joe's personality is revealed by his readiness to make judgements and generalisations about others. In 'Water Them Geraniums', his anecdotes about Mrs Spicer are interspersed with such pronouncements as: 'They had a sense of the ridiculous, most of these poor sundried Bushwomen' (p.159), and 'Most Bushwomen get the nagging habit' (p.163). In this way, the narrative develops its portrait of Mrs Spicer, while also consolidating Joe's character. Such remarks demonstrate Joe's sense that he and his family are slightly superior to their neighbours, reinforced by his assertion that 'We were the aristocrats of Lahey's Creek' (p.162).

## Women

**Key quotes**

'Her surroundings are not favourable to the development of the 'womanly' or sentimental side of nature' ('The Drover's Wife', p.25)

'[S]he was a gaunt, haggard Bushwoman…' ('Water Them Geraniums', p.149)

'She has a keen, very keen, sense of the ridiculous...' ('The Drover's Wife', p.25)

There are several significant, strong women characters in Lawson's fiction; amongst the stories set for study, these include the drover's wife, Mary Wilson, Mrs Spicer and Brighten's sister-in-law. Other, relatively minor women characters that nevertheless play important roles are

Mrs Baker and her sister, Miss Standish, in 'Telling Mrs Baker'; and the wife, Emma, in 'A Child in the Dark'.

### The 'gaunt, haggard Bushwoman'

Mrs Spicer is an extreme instance of the 'type' represented, in more sympathetic forms, in the characters of the drover's wife and, to a lesser degree, Mary Wilson — the 'gaunt, haggard Bushwoman'. These women share the capacity to survive in adverse circumstances, yet they are also vulnerable to the damaging effects (as Lawson represents them) of life in the bush. On the whole, they are resigned to the misfortunes and difficulties of their lives, and they never stop caring for their families or being generous in their friendships. They have the strength to take on onerous tasks, but also take pleasure in the society and culture of the town (as opposed to the bush), such as 'dressing up' or the 'fashion-plates' of women's magazines.

Of these women, Mary Wilson is the most ambitious in terms of seeking improvements in the quality of her life. Her aspirations, as 'A Double Buggy at Lahey's Creek' suggests, are realistic, and she displays the commitment and capacity to work towards achieving them. Mary is also the least affected by the rigours of bush life, though Joe sees the early signs of her physical decline: 'her cheeks were getting thin, and the colour was going' ('A Double Buggy at Lahey's Creek', p.135).

Mary's habit of dressing up on Sunday afternoons and having the family walk along the creek recalls that of the drover's wife in Lawson's earlier story, and sets them both apart from Mrs Spicer. In 'The Drover's Wife' it is clear that this 'dressing up' constitutes a means of differentiating at least one day in the week (Sunday) from all the others, thus breaking up the monotony of bush life. The Spicers are prevented from dressing in better clothes by their extreme poverty; however, Mrs Spicer's recognition of the social importance of dress codes is reflected in Joe's observation that her children 'were always as clean and tidy as possible when they came to our place' ('Water Them Geraniums', p.161).

The connections between Mrs Spicer and the 'drover's wife' are made explicit in a number of ways, including the repetition of key phrases in the narratives, emphasising that these women represent 'types' rather than unique individuals. In 'Water Them Geraniums', the accounts of Mrs Spicer treating her cows for pleuro-pneumonia and beating back a fire on her property recall incidents in 'The Drover's Wife', as does her story about putting her fingers through holes in her handkerchief (pp.159 and 25 respectively). These episodes demonstrate the women's self-reliance and shared 'sense of the ridiculous', qualities not unique to themselves but in common with, as Joe Wilson puts it, 'most of those poor sundried Bushwomen' (p.159).

### The Practical Generosity of Bushwomen

The nurturing capacities of Lawson's bushwomen often seem to be compromised by the amount of physical, outdoors work they perform, but they are generous with their time and their resources. Mrs Spicer's generosity is evident in her early gift to the Wilsons of fresh meat, and in the way she helps Mary when the Wilsons' second child is born. Her practical nature is shown by her inclination to find a task to do rather than engage in conversation. Brighten's sister-in-law displays a similar efficiency, wasting little time on words once she sees what must be done to save Joe's child.

Mary suggests that Mrs Spicer might have been 'fairly well brought up' (p.162), in which case her present circumstances represent a significant decline in living standards. Her reluctance to visit the relatively comfortable Wilson household too often, since 'I git the dismals afterwards' (p.162), indicates she is not so much ignorant as determined to accept her own situation and not dwell on her misfortunes. This is another trait that Mrs Spicer shares with the drover's wife and Brighten's sister-in-law, both of whom are living in more impoverished circumstances than they had previously enjoyed, but who are more or less reconciled to their lot.

### Emotional Restraint

In contrast to Lawson's male characters, the women share a tendency to show emotions openly — to weep, or even scream. The way in which Mary Wilson screams, according to Joe, is 'how a woman cries out when her child is in danger or dying — short, and sharp, and terrible' ('Brighten's Sister-in-Law', p.104). Mitchell recalls that his mother 'screamed and nearly fainted when she saw me' ('On the Edge of a Plain', p.61), a sign of her over-reaction, as he represents it, to his unexpected reappearance.

Lawson's women characters cry far more readily than his male characters. For instance, the drover's wife recalls several tearful occasions, and 'tears spring to her eyes' when she realises her woodpile is 'built hollow' (p.25). However, she is not shown to scream, even when the snake emerges. In fact, the narratives typically express most admiration for women characters when they are able to show emotional restraint. In 'The Drover's Wife', the woman 'does not gush or make a fuss about it' when her husband returns (p.25). The narrative suggests that this trait is partly a response to her situation, since her 'surroundings are not favourable to the development of the 'womanly' or sentimental side of nature' (p.25). However, the narrator exclaims at her interest in fashion: 'Heaven help her!' (p.22). In this way, the narrative conveys an implicit approval of the woman's lack of 'womanliness'; of the kind of women the bush is 'favourable to the development of'.

Similarly, in 'Brighten's Sister-in-Law', Joe remarks on the woman's being 'handsome', which is not a characteristically feminine quality, and she also seems in other ways to be in between femininity and masculinity. She cries, but only sheds 'two great tears' and then quickly resumes self-control, restoring her facial expression to 'the same as before the tears' (p.120). This self-control seems all the more impressive due to the woman's apparent intensity of feeling, indicated by Joe's estimation that he 'never saw a woman's eyes so haggard and hopeless' (p.120).

### Alternative Women

A quite different representation of a woman who lives in the bush on a struggling selection is Emma in 'A Child in the Dark'. Her interests in writing and reading are not represented positively, but in terms of an unreasonable neglect of domestic and maternal responsibilities. As a wife and mother, she is cast as having a misplaced set of priorities that places almost impossible demands on her family. Unlike the women previously considered, Emma is far from reconciled to her situation, complaining about being 'chained to a man who can't say a word of truth!' and living in a 'wretched hole' (pp.216, 217). In fact, it is Emma whom the narrative shows to be a persistent liar. She lacks the inclination to make her circumstances more pleasant, and does not seem to have any means of transcending, or even escaping, her situation.

In this sense, Mary Wilson, who is also frustrated by her circumstances, is represented in a more positive light. Mary is evidently prepared and able to work hard in order to improve her family's situation; Joe acknowledges that 'She had tried to help me to better things ... She used to plan a lot' (p.144). Mary's capacity not merely to plan but also to accomplish is demonstrated by the success of the potato crop in 'A Double Buggy at Lahey's Creek'. In contrast, Emma in 'A Child in the Dark' is focused on her own world, represented by the bedroom in which she remains confined throughout the story. Unlike Mary Wilson, Emma shows little concern for the welfare of her family as a whole.

Miss Standish in 'Telling Mrs Baker' represents another version of womanhood; her difference from those around her devolves largely from her living in the city and being identified with city tastes and lifestyles. As such, she is discussed in more detail in the 'City and the Bush' section of **Themes & issues**.

## Relationships: Male Mateship

### Key quotes

'"How could I face his wife if I went home without him?" asked Andy, "or any of his old mates?"' ('Telling Mrs Baker', p.198)

'I'd do as much for yer an' more than any other man, an' well yer knows it...' ('The Bush Undertaker', p.31)

'[I]t isn't Bush religion to desert a mate in a hole; and the Boss was a mate of ours; so we stuck to him' ('Telling Mrs Baker', p.198)

### Key point

Male mateship is a central element in the bush mythology associated with the literature of Lawson, Paterson, Furphy and other (male) *Bulletin* writers. In general, Lawson's male characters value and demonstrate an unceasing loyalty to their mates, although these relationships are not sentimental or romantic. As Jack, the narrator of 'Telling Mrs Baker', puts it, mateship constitutes a form of

'Bush religion' in Lawson's stories, but in Australian society it has also become a kind of nationalist 'religion', as in the Anzac tradition or various national sporting endeavours.

### Bob Baker: the Test of Mateship

One male character whose behaviour does not live up to these ideals, and who thereby represents the consequences of betraying the codes of mateship, is Bob Baker. The story hints at the significant stresses that droving could place on family relationships, since the trip undertaken is a 'two years' trip' from New South Wales to the Gulf of Carpentaria in far northern Australia (p.196). The importance of mateship in such circumstances lies in its guarantee of support and solidarity between men who are away from their families and sources of material comfort for extended periods.

Bob betrays his mates, as well as his marriage, by seeking comfort and solace in alcohol and the company of other women. These are short-term pleasures only, and lead to his emotional and physical decline. The droving trip stalls and Bob is sacked, leaving Andy and Jack without work and eventually with the predicament of dealing with the consequences of Bob's death. When Andy examines Bob's papers, he finds letters from several other women, including 'other men's wives'; Andy is particularly disgusted to find that 'one of those men ... was an old mate of his!' (p.201), thus asserting a rough equivalence between the betrayal of mateship and the betrayal of marriage.

Andy asserts and demonstrates the values of mateship even when his loyalties are tested. He refuses to drink with Bob, due to a promise he has made to Mrs Baker. Andy's loyalty to Mrs Baker strongly influences his actions, suggesting that some of the attributes of mateship can also extend to male-female friendships. Mostly, though, mateship in Lawson refers to relationships between men. Andy is particularly aware of how other men, Bob's 'old mates', would regard him if he doesn't remain loyal to Bob (p.198), indicating that mateship involves an extended network of relationships and associations, of mutual expectations and obligations.

Andy's determination to remain with Bob minimises the harmful effects of Bob's actions on his wife. Andy also invokes the code of mateship to convince Jack to assist him in 'telling Mrs Baker' a false story about Bob's death: 'you're surely not crawler enough to desert a mate in a case like this?' he asks, not giving Jack any real choice in the matter (p.199). He affirms the necessity of telling such a story by insisting that: 'we've got a dead mate to consider as well as a living woman' (p.200), perpetuating the bonds of mateship beyond death.

### Other Mateship Bonds

In 'The Loaded Dog', the mates Andy, Jim and Dave form a close-knit working unit. They demonstrate a willingness not only to work together but also to share a camp and each other's company for many hours in each day. They roster the duties and make the most of their complementary talents; their mix of ideas and practical know-how is suggested by such remarks as:

> Andy usually put Dave's theories into practice if they were practicable, or bore the blame for the failure and the chaffing of his mates if they weren't (p.95).

The banter and camaraderie between the men is readily apparent, reinforcing the lack of sentimentality in mateship bonds and relationships.

In 'On the Edge of a Plain' Mitchell is accompanied by 'his mate' in their trek across the plain. Between these two mates the relationship is not as strongly defined as, say, that between Andy and Jack in 'Telling Mrs Baker', although its nuances are subtly explored in a sequence of several story-sketches in While the Billy Boils. In 'On the Edge of a Plain' the mate does little apart from respond to aspects of Mitchell's yarn, yet there is a sense of the two men's readiness to share possessions and stories, and of the reassurance they gain from each other's companionship.

### Men Who Live and Work Alone

Although mateship is a feature of the relationships between male characters in several of the stories, an equally interesting aspect of Lawson's representations of men is how isolated from contact with other men (not to mention women) they usually are. Some of the stories' most striking images are of solitary men: Joe Wilson desperately riding for help while cradling his unconscious son in 'Brighten's Sister-in-Law'; the bush undertaker improvising a burial service for his mate Brummy; the union worker 'James Tyson' who dies while taking horses across the Darling in 'The Union Buries Its Dead'.

**Key point**

In these stories, loneliness is a virtually inevitable consequence of living in the bush, and Lawson emphasises its effects, especially on men, by examining the mental and emotional states of isolated male characters. Their ability to cope with isolation and loneliness is a sign of their self-reliance; at the same time, their struggle with these things reflects the harshness of their existence and the anti-romantic qualities of Lawson's bush.

## Relationships: Women and Men

**Key quotes**

'[Mary] tried to make a gentleman of me for years, but gave it up gradually' ('Water Them Geraniums', p.152)

'She is glad when her husband returns, but she does not gush or make a fuss about it' ('The Drover's Wife', p.25)

'It seems, now, as though we had been sweethearts long years before, and had parted, and had never really met since' ('Water Them Geraniums', p.145)

Lawson represents relationships between men and women as uneasy, characterised by differences or misunderstandings between individuals, by conflict rather than tenderness. The male characters share a sense of being very different to women, unable to see the world as women see it and determined to maintain their own sphere of interests and power. A comic example of this tension occurs in 'Bill, The Ventriloquial Rooster', when Mitchell's father and his mates take advantage of the 'old lady and the girls' being away in order to stage a cockfight (p.75). Their assumption is that not only will the women be uninterested in the fight, but they will be angry with the men for holding it — a well-founded assumption it turns out; Mitchell's father 'had a lively old time with the old lady afterwards' (p.77).

The women, on the other hand, typically show commitment and loyalty to their relationships with male characters. Mrs Baker asserts that her husband was 'one of the kindest men that ever lived', which partly explains why she is so willing to believe Andy's fabricated story about Bob's death ('Telling Mrs Baker', p.206). However, Bob Baker's behaviour demonstrates his minimal commitment to the marriage and that his 'loyalty' was chiefly to his own experiences of pleasure. The husband in 'The Drover's Wife' is characterised as 'careless, but a good enough husband' (p.22); when he returns from droving it is the wife who attends to his needs and 'gets him something good to eat' (p.25) rather than he who attends to her.

### Marriages

Lawson represents marriages as full of difficulties but lasting, nevertheless — due mostly to the efforts of the wife. The marriage between Joe and Mary Wilson has moments of intimacy and affection, but the dominant notes are of tension and estrangement: 'what strangers we were to each other', Joe remarks in 'Water Them Geraniums' (p.145). The different temperaments and expectations of Mary and Joe are evident throughout the quartet, as in Joe's admission that Mary 'tried to make a gentleman of me for years, but gave it up gradually' (p.152). The overall pattern of the Wilsons' marriage is of initial hopefulness, then increasing disenchantment and divergent interests.

This pattern is also evident in the marriage of the Wilsons' neighbours, the Spicers. Mrs Spicer reflects that in the early years 'Spicer was a very different man then to what he is now' (p.160), and her complaint about Spicer's tendency to be 'moody and gloomy ... he hardly ever speaks' (p.160) echoes Mary's similar remarks about Joe. Of course, at the end of 'A Double Buggy at Lahey's Creek' Mary and Joe talk 'more than we'd done for years' (p.141), suggesting that the tensions between married couples need not be irreconcilable.

The marriage in 'A Child in the Dark, and a Foreign Father' is the most strained of all marriages in these stories. The wife, frustrated with her circumstances, rebukes her husband at every opportunity and complains, unreasonably it seems, about his 'infernal lies' and 'everlasting growling' (pp.216, 219). The roles taken up by husband and wife in this marriage are in many ways the reverse of those in other Lawson's stories, since Nils takes responsibility for the care of the children and household chores, while Emma seems concerned only for her own well-being and pleasures. There seems to be no possible resolution to the tensions in this marriage, and of course in the case of Lawson's parents, as with Lawson's own marriage, the result was a separation between husband and wife. Interestingly, none of the stories set for study actually represents such a separation between husband and wife, although on the whole Lawson certainly depicts marriage in negative, pessimistic terms.

# THEMES & ISSUES

## The City and the Bush

**Key quotes**

'If he had the means he would take her to the city and keep her there like a princess' ('The Drover's Wife', p.22)

'There's no timber in the world so ghostly as the Australian Bush in moonlight — or just about daybreak' ('Brighten's Sister-in-Law', p.116)

'[T]he old shepherd, though used to the weird and dismal, as one living alone in the bush must necessarily be, felt the icy breath of fear at his heart' ('The Bush Undertaker', p.32)

'Sounds queer to you city people, doesn't it?' ('Telling Mrs Baker', p.199)

The vast difference between the city and the bush is a persistent theme in Lawson's fiction. The stories set for study deploy bush or outback locations; they feature characters who feel at home in the bush, who rarely visit the city and who endorse the values and cultures of the bush over those of the city. Nevertheless, Lawson's representation of bush life is a complex one, highlighting its harshness and monotony, depicting the flaws as well as the virtues of its inhabitants.

In 'Telling Mrs Baker' Jack indicates his awareness of the differences between city and bush cultures. He approvingly describes Ned's fight with the publican following Bob's death, and the policemen's support for Ned. He then directly addresses the reader: 'Sounds queer to you city people, doesn't it?' (p.199). Jack is aware that these moral codes are unconventional by city standards, but he nonetheless endorses them. This remark also indicates that Jack, and by extension Lawson, imagines the story's readers to be inhabitants of the city, rather than the bush.

### The 'weird and dismal' Bush

Even from the perspective of Lawson's bushmen and women, the bush is not represented as *entirely* comforting. It is frequently characterised as weird and ghostly, and as causing its inhabitants to experience intense loneliness and the risk of madness. Joe Wilson's observations of these qualities in the bush partly reflect his own melancholic disposition. In 'Brighten's Sister-in-Law', the bush seems to be 'sighing' (p.111), then to be 'full of ghosts' when Joe perceives his son to be close to death (p.116). On the first morning on the Lahey's Creek selection, in 'Water Them Geraniums', Joe feels that the bush looks 'brighter' after the tense, previous night, his own mood seeming to match perfectly that of the surrounding country.

## Key point

The bush is shown to produce eccentric qualities in its inhabitants, especially those who lack regular company. Joe Wilson suggests that 'most men who have been alone in the Bush for any length of time — and married couples too — are more or less mad' ('Water Them Geraniums', p.151). The 'bush undertaker' is the clearest example of a man who has become thoroughly 'used to the weird and dismal' (p.32), and the bush is cast as the 'nurse and tutor of eccentric minds' (p.34); the landscape is not merely a backdrop for events, but an active force in them.

Overall, Lawson represents bush life as producing admirable qualities, such as generosity, self-reliance and contentment with modest pleasures and comforts. At the end of 'A Double Buggy at Lahey's Creek', the Wilsons' new buggy is laden with gifts including a ham, loaves of bread and 'a fresh-water cod, that long Dave Regan had caught' (p.140). This evokes a picture of an extended bush community, people with few resources but generous in spirit, able to give items of real value and usefulness.

### Men and Women Not Equally at Home in the Bush

The affinity of Lawson's characters for the bush is more evident for the men than the women. Whereas the men are most at ease in the bush, women cope with bush life while also having a fondness for the city. In 'The Drover's Wife' the husband would, if he 'had the means', take his wife 'to the city and keep her there like a princess' (p.22). This suggests that the city is a space of luxury and comfort but the husband would only move there for his wife's pleasure, not his own. In 'Water Them Geraniums', Mary pleads to Joe to 'take me away from the Bush', but Joe does not consider this as a serious possibility (p.166). Joe perceives the city to be a place where 'every comfort that a woman could ask for' is available — that is, where women, rather than men, experience pleasure ('A Double Buggy at Lahey's Creek', p.134).

In 'Telling Mrs Baker' Miss Standish is from the city but finds herself temporarily in the bush. Jack characterises her as:

> a Sydney girl … fresh and fair — not like the sun-browned women we were used to see.… She had her hair done and was dressed in the city style.… (p.203)

Jack and Andy, the tough drover mates, become shy and awkward in the face of feminine city style and beauty. Moreover, Miss Standish 'had been educated' and 'wrote stories for the Sydney *Bulletin* and other Sydney papers' (p.203). This, perhaps more than any other attribute, sets Miss Standish apart from Lawson's bushwomen: she performs work for which she is paid. At the end of the story, Miss Standish expresses her admiration of 'the Bushmen! They are grand men — they are noble' (p.208). Yet the story suggests that there is little that is grand or noble about the two men, and Miss Standish, despite her city sophistication, ultimately is able only to comprehend and express her admiration for them in clichéd terms.

### Brighten's Sister-in-law: Bridging the Gap between City and Bush

Brighten's sister-in-law is the only character who bridges the gap between the city and the bush, who is familiar with and able to inhabit both worlds. She had been 'a hospital matron in the city' (p.115), and her professional expertise is evident in her prompt and effective treatment of Jim. Moreover, her appreciation of 'civilised' social forms is suggested by her setting the table as Joe 'seldom saw it set out there' (p.121). Joe's admiration is due both to her description of 'Sydney and Sydney life as I'd never heard it described before', and also her knowledge of 'the Bush and old digging days' (p.121). She is as practical and resourceful as any of Lawson's bushmen and women, even though she is clearly not of their type; she is as competent with words and 'quick to understand' as Miss Standish, but without the younger woman's tendency to romanticise the bush.

Brighten's sister-in-law suggests that the difference between the city and the bush does not preclude the possibility of moving between them, but it is clear that the ability to be equally at home in either space requires 'a woman out of the ordinary' (p.115) — a woman, in fact, who is unlike any other character in Lawson's fiction.

## Selectors and Squatters

**Key quotes**

'I rode across to Wall's station and tackled the old man; but he was a hard man.... I was a selector and that was enough for him' ('Water Them Geraniums', p.166)

'He was a drover, and started squatting here when they were married. The drought of 18 — ruined him' ('The Drover's Wife', pp.21–22)

'I made up my mind to take on a small selection farm ... at a place called Lahey's Creek' ('Brighten's Sister-in-Law', p.108)

Lawson knew about the lives of selectors from personal experience, and they feature in many of his stories. He grew up on a selection near Mudgee, like the family in 'A Child in the Dark'; Joe Wilson takes up a selection at 'Lahey's Creek' in roughly the same stretch of country. Jack Mitchell recalls his childhood 'up-country on the selection' in 'Bill, the Ventriloquial Rooster' (p.73). Selectors faced difficulties due to the poor soil on which they attempted to farm and to natural phenomena such as droughts and floods. The selectors' struggle was one of the contributing factors in the rise of the notion of 'mateship', since only the cooperative efforts of individuals would enable them to survive.

Squatters faced difficulties too, but they were far better resourced than selectors and acquired better quality land in the first place. Nevertheless, many squatters failed due to the depression and the long drought in the eastern colonies during the 1890s. The husband in 'The Drover's Wife' is a squatter, but returned to droving when 'The drought of 18 — ruined him' (p.22). In 'Telling Mrs Baker', Bob Baker is an ex-squatter who 'went under' after 'a pretty severe drought' (p.196), although Jack also suggests that Bob had been too careless with his money in times of success.

### Squatters' Control of the Land

Lawson represents squatters as tending to make things difficult for selectors and drovers. 'Water Them Geraniums', alludes to the squatters' practice of placing 'dummy' selectors on crown land in order to use it themselves: Joe Wilson wonders whether his neighbour, Spicer, 'wasn't a selector at all, only a 'dummy' for the squatter of the Cobborah run' (p.156). Drovers also come into conflict with squatters; in 'Telling Mrs Baker', the narrator refers to the need to move across the squatters' runs as quickly as possible: 'we had to keep the bullocks moving along the route all the time, or else get into trouble for trespass' (p.197).

Joe Wilson refers to the squatters' use of 'all manner of dodges and paltry persecution' (p.156), and the narrative point of view throughout Lawson's fiction is generally unsympathetic to the squatters. They are not fleshed-out characters, but shadowy figures, remote from the everyday struggles of selectors and drovers. A good example is the indifference of the squatter, Wall, to Mrs Spicer's desperate circumstances, which his actions have needlessly exacerbated. Joe asks Wall for sympathy in the case of Billy Spicer, who has been arrested for stealing one of Wall's horses. However, Joe despairs that Wall 'wouldn't listen to me ... I was a selector and that was enough for him' ('Water Them Geraniums', p.166).

## Death

**Key quotes**

'It was some time before we could believe that she was dead' ('Water Them Geraniums', p.167)

'He turned it over on its side; it fell flat on its back like a board, and the shrivelled eyes seemed to peer up at him from under the blackened wrists' ('The Bush Undertaker', p.29)

'We were all strangers to the corpse' ('The Union Buries Its Dead', p.41)

One of the features of the bush landscape in Lawson's stories is the proximity to death of its inhabitants. Lawson's characters are regularly exposed to the appearance and effects of death, and untimely deaths occur all too frequently. In 'The Drover's Wife' there are recollections of the deaths of children and of the 'two best cows' (p.23), and of the appearance of 'a gallows-faced swagman' (p.24). Mrs Spicer has similar confrontations with death in 'Water Them Geraniums', and the story ends with her own death. The 'bush undertaker' investigates burial sites as a form of recreation, and performs an impromptu burial service for his old mate, Brummy. Another burial is at the centre of 'The Union Buries Its Dead', which questions the meaning and dignity of human life and death in a cynical, yet meditative fashion.

### Death 'in the horrors'

One category of wandering bushmen who always represent a threat, and yet seem close to death themselves, are those who are half-mad from alcohol. Some men turn to drink for comfort and relief, then finally die 'in the horrors'. This is the fate of Brummy in 'The Bush Undertaker', Bob Baker in 'Telling Mrs Baker' and an anonymous bushman in 'Water Them Geraniums'. In the latter case, Mrs Spicer gives the man a large amount of coffee one morning, before he walks off with 'two saddle-straps in his hands' (p.164). Tommy Spicer finds him hanging from a tree, and the sight both fascinates and appalls the children.

In 'The Bush Undertaker', the old man guesses that Brummy had died 'early in his spree' (p.29), and jokes to the corpse about how 'the rum as preserved yer' (p.30). Alcohol may lead to 'the horrors', but Lawson's stories also indicate that it was an accepted, and even necessary part of the bush lifestyle. Joe Wilson reflects on how the prospect of a 'periodical spree' could keep isolated shepherds and boundary riders committed to their jobs: 'Drink is the only break in the awful monotony' ('Water Them Geraniums', p.151). The central place of drinking establishments in outback towns is also foregrounded in 'The Union Buries Its Dead', in which the funeral 'gathered at a corner pub' (p.40).

### Symbols of Life and Death

Although 'The Union Buries Its Dead' purports to be a realistic description of the burial of an anonymous man in an outback town, a number of features of the narrative give the story its wider, universal significance. The repetition of key words and the loaded nature of certain images suggest that they operate on a symbolic as well as a literal level.

An early example of repetition is the use of the phrase 'passed away'. This phrase ostensibly describes the passing of time by people in the pub, but since many of them are waiting for a funeral the other meaning of 'passed away' — of having died — is also present. The implication is that their drinking and dancing, and then 'skylarking and fighting', are indicative of how they pass their lives in general, without real meaning or passion (p.40). After they have passed their lives in this way, they too will 'pass away', perhaps, like the young union labourer, with few people to care about their passing.

In this context, a phrase like 'respect for the dead' is heavily ironic. 'Respect' recurs a number of times in the narrative, drawing the reader's attention to how superficial this 'respect' is. The pubs close their front doors out of respect — but the side and back entrances remain open. The drunk shearers take off their hats as the funeral procession passes, but the 'respect for the departed' this suggests is undercut by the narrator's sarcastic 'whoever he might have been', implying the gesture is devoid of any real feeling (p.41).

A key image in this story is that of the drops of water sprinkled on the coffin: they 'quickly evaporated, and the little round black spots they left were soon dusted over' (p.42). Of course, this image conveys the heat and dryness of the air, but the phrase 'dusted over' also echoes the phrase from the traditional burial service: 'earth to earth, ashes to ashes, dust to dust'. In Lawson's image, the water drops are symbolic of the fleeting, transient nature of human life, which turns all too swiftly into dust — not just in the outback, but in all places and at all times.

The burial ceremony performed by the old man in 'The Bush Undertaker' is less formally correct but far more deeply felt. The shepherd's genuine 'respect for the dead' is indicated by such phrases as 'a flood of memories, in which the old man became absorbed' (p.33), and his removal of his hat to place it 'carefully on the grass' (p.34). The old man's sincerity and respect for the dignity of his dead mate are in stark contrast to the occasion narrated in 'The Union Buries Its Dead', and thus the narrative suggests that the old man himself, for all his eccentricity, retains his dignity.

## Women's Roles

### Key quotes

'There are things that a bushwoman cannot do' ('The Drover's Wife', p.23)

'I thought of Mary, outside in the blazing heat ... doing the work of a station manager as well as that of a housewife and mother' ('A Double Buggy at Lahey's Creek', p.135)

In the way they describe the severe physical decline women suffer as a result of performing outdoor, manual work, and in the way they describe the disorder and stresses prevailing in families when the husband/father is absent, Lawson's stories suggest that certain roles are inappropriate for women. They imply that a woman's proper place lies within the home, performing 'appropriate' womanly duties.

As a result of their harsh circumstances, women characters lose their physical beauty, and (perhaps more significantly, from Joe Wilson's point of view) they become increasingly eccentric and antisocial. The harshness of the Spicers' lives in 'Water Them Geraniums' is embodied in the figure of Mrs Spicer:

> gaunt and flat-chested, and her face was 'burnt to a brick'.... She had ... a sharp face — ground sharp by hardship — and the cheeks drawn in.... She was not more than forty. (p.157)

Here the narrative conveys the stresses of the bush life in terms of a premature loss of feminine beauty, whereas for men the bush only seems to enhance their masculine virtues. In this way, the reader's attention is drawn not so much to the characters' material circumstances as to the 'appropriateness' to their gender of the roles they undertake.

#### Women Wearing Men's Clothes

One of the signs of a confusion of gender roles in the bush is a woman wearing her husband's clothes while undertaking outdoor tasks. In 'The Drover's Wife', the woman fights a fire while wearing 'an old pair of her husband's trousers'. This causes her son Tommy to laugh, but the woman's neglect of her 'proper', motherly duties is then emphasised by the phrase 'the terrified baby howled lustily for his 'mummy'' (p.23).

In 'A Double Buggy at Lahey's Creek' Mary wears Joe's 'new pair of 'lastic-side boots' when in the paddocks; Joe remarks that she 'generally got them off before I got home' (p.127). One infers that Mary's action is a kind of disobedience because it crosses gender boundaries. Joe's work as a carrier, and the drover's work, takes them away from their households for extended periods, compromising their wives' capacity to devote themselves to domestic chores and the nurturing of their children. Thus the men's absence is represented as causing a blurring of the separation between men's and women's domains and activities, a blurring couched in negative terms (such as the loss of 'womanliness'), rather than in positive ones.

## Key point

The gender politics of Lawson's stories are thus quite conservative. Although written at a time when women were making significant social, material and political gains, the stories advocate the maintenance of the status quo. In 'The Drover's Wife' the woman's husband is mostly absent and she is represented as both vulnerable and resourceful. However, her identity is largely determined by her relationship to her husband: the narrative knows her as the 'drover's wife', not by her own name. She is able to cope on her own, but at every stage the narrative emphasises the difficulties she faces due to her husband's absence. The narrative asserts that 'There are things that a bushwoman cannot do' (p.23), implying that a man could do these things — and ought to be doing them.

### Woman as Mother

The role of mother in Lawsons' stories is simultaneously highly valued, and closely scrutinised. Both the drover's wife and Mrs Spicer are represented as rather harsh mothers, who struggle to maintain a balance between domestic discipline and the expression of tenderness and love. Joe Wilson comments on what he perceives to be 'the nagging habit' in bushwomen, which he observes in Mrs Spicer's 'everlastingly nagging at the children' ('Water Them Geraniums', p.163). This tendency in the mother signals frustration with a life of limited opportunities and variety, but also, and perhaps more powerfully, a weakness of character.

Joe Wilson compares the 'nagging habit' unfavourably with 'the drinking habit in a father' (p.163), implying that 'nagging' is exclusively a fault in women. This is echoed by the narrative of 'A Child in the Dark', in which Emma seems to 'nag' her husband and children, whereas Nils is quietly attentive to his family's needs. The narrator of 'The Drover's Wife' indicates that, to the woman's children, 'she seems harsh' (p.25); the woman is evidently a capable and caring mother, yet the narrative suggests her lack of tenderness is also a kind of inadequacy.

Brighten's sister-in-law seems to have the qualities of discipline and tenderness in abundance, but her happiness and sense of fulfilment appear to suffer due to her lack of children — her inability, that is, to perform the role of 'mother'. Her 'haggard, hungry, hopeless look' (p.122) is apparently brought to the surface by her experience of bringing Jim through his fever. Joe sees her 'two great tears' when she nurses Jim (p.120), then when they leave 'tears came into her eyes' (p.122). She forms a close bond with Jim in very little time, showing her nurturing, motherly qualities to be abundant; what she lacks is her own child, without which, it seems, her 'hopeless' look will remain with her indefinitely.

## National Identity and Race

### Key quotes

'Her husband is an Australian, and so is she' ('The Drover's Wife', p.22)

'I have left out the 'sad Australian sunset' because the sun was not going down at the time' ('The Union Buries Its Dead', p.42)

The issue of Australian national identity is continually at stake in Lawson's stories. They are concerned with Australian settings and characters, and display no interest in cultures or events outside of Australia. The *Bulletin* writers and editors held that Australia's identity was most evident not in the cities but in the bush, where the circumstances and values that were uniquely and characteristically Australian had been brought into being, and Lawson's stories are completely consistent with this position.

Unfortunately, such a version of Australia's national identity marginalises or excludes more 'Australians' than it includes. The seminomadic, itinerant bush workers mythologised by such writers as Lawson, Paterson and Furphy were white men. Lawson's characters and narrators display a patronising attitude towards members of other races or nationalities. Also, women are represented as not quite the equals of men, and are mostly relegated to the powerless domains of the kitchen or bedroom (the place of the 'confinement' during pregnancy).

### Aboriginal Identities and White Australia

Aboriginal people are never regarded as 'Australians' in Lawson's stories. For instance, in 'The Drover's Wife', the narrator states that 'Her husband is an Australian, and so is she' (p.22). This simply makes the point that he was born in Australia — which was sometimes referred to as being 'native born'. Of course, Aboriginal people were born in Australia too, but the characters 'Black Mary', 'King Jimmy' and a 'stray blackfellow' are represented as inferior to the drover and his wife, and as outside the category of 'Australians'.

The most telling anecdote is of the woodpile, built by the 'stray blackfellow', which turns out to be hollow (p.25). This story repeats the stereotype of the black person as lazy and unreliable. The adjective 'stray' suggests the man lacks a proper place of his own, which is an arrogant presumption on the part of the narrator — ignoring both the nomadic lifestyle of Aboriginal people and the dispossession of their traditional lands by white colonisers. There is also an allusion to the notion of the 'dying race' in the phrase 'He was the last of his tribe and a King' (p.25).

Lawson never introduces an Aboriginal character — stereotyped either as 'black' or 'half-caste' — without indicating that he or she is somehow lacking in intelligence or ability. In 'The Loaded Dog', for instance, 'a half-caste rush[es] aimlessly round with a dipper of cold water' (p.100). The narrator does not consider it necessary even to gender this character, whose inept confusion contrasts with the helpless laughter of the white bushmen and women. It seems, in fact, that the 'half-caste' character has more in common with the uncomprehending flight of the dogs. She or he is an entirely unnecessary element in the story, and only emphasises Lawson's willingness to mock or patronise Aboriginal people.

In 'A Double Buggy at Lahey's Creek', the Wilsons' 'black boy' is a similarly pathetic figure, 'sidling along by the wall, as if he were afraid somebody was going to hit him — poor little devil!' (p.139). His narrative function is simply to tell Mary and Joe that the buggy is coming, adding to the sense of anticipation as the story reaches its climax. Joe promises to 'tell ... about him some other time' (p.139), but at this point the story is almost concluded, and the 'black boy' remains a mostly silent, peripheral figure, consigned to the margins of white settlement and pleasure. Thus, these Aboriginal characters testify to the existence of a bush hierarchy, in which black people are subservient to whites and accept their places in this structure quite amicably.

## Key point

Lawson's fiction reflects the ideas, prevalent in his lifetime, that Aboriginal people were incapable of being taught to work productively and had no future. These ideas were also reflected in and perpetuated by government policies such as the 'White Australia' policy. Moreover, these stories refuse to acknowledge the violent and unlawful means by which white people occupied the land, and the strength of Aboriginal resistance to colonisation.

# QUESTIONS & ANSWERS

This section focuses on your own analytical writing on Lawson's short stories, and gives you strategies for producing high-quality responses in your coursework and exam essays.

In writing on a collection of short stories, your response will depend crucially on which stories you focus on. Try to balance detailed reference to two or three stories with your display of knowledge of the collection as a whole. Don't discuss the stories individually as if they are completely isolated from each other, but move confidently between stories, showing connections between them as well as variations and points of difference.

## Essay writing – an overview

An essay on a literary work is a formal and serious piece of writing that presents your point of view on the text, usually in response to a given essay topic. Your 'point of view' in an essay is your interpretation of the meaning of the text's language, structure, characters, situations and events, supported by detailed analysis of textual evidence.

### Analyse – don't summarise

In your essays it is important to avoid simply summarising what happens in a text.

- A **summary** is a description or paraphrase (retelling in different words) of the characters and events. For example: 'Macbeth has a horrifying vision of a dagger dripping with blood before he goes to murder King Duncan.'
- An **analysis** is an explanation of the real meaning or significance that lies 'beneath' the text's words (and images, for a film). For example: 'Macbeth's vision of a bloody dagger shows how deeply uneasy he is about the violent act he is contemplating – as well as his sense that supernatural forces are impelling him to act.'

A limited amount of summary is sometimes necessary to let your reader know which part of the text you wish to discuss. However, always keep this to a minimum and follow it immediately with your analysis of what this part of the text is really telling us.

### Plan your essay

Carefully plan your essay so that you have a clear idea of what you are going to say. The plan ensures that your ideas flow logically, that your argument remains consistent and that you stay on the topic. An essay plan should be a list of **brief dot points** – no more than half a page.

- Include your central argument or main contention – a concise statement (usually in a single sentence) of your overall response to the topic. See 'Analysing a sample topic' for guidelines on how to formulate a main contention.
- Write three or four dot points for each paragraph indicating the main idea and evidence/examples from the text. Note that in your essay you will need to *expand* on these points and *analyse* the evidence.

### Structure your essay

An essay is a complete, self-contained piece of writing. It has a clear beginning (the introduction), middle (several body paragraphs) and end (the last paragraph or conclusion). It must also have a central argument that runs throughout, linking each paragraph to form a coherent whole.

See examples of introductions and conclusions in the 'Analysing a sample topic' and 'Sample answer' sections.

**The introduction establishes your overall response to the topic.** It includes your main contention and outlines the main evidence you will refer to in the course of the essay. Write your introduction *after* you have done a plan and *before* you write the rest of the essay.

**The body paragraphs argue your case** – they present evidence from the text and explain how this evidence supports your argument. Each body paragraph needs:

- a strong **topic sentence** (usually the first sentence) that states the main point being made in the paragraph
- **evidence** from the text, including some brief quotations

- **analysis** of the textual evidence explaining its significance and **explanation** of how it supports your argument
- **links back to the topic** in one or more statements, usually towards the end of the paragraph.

Connect the body paragraphs so that your discussion flows smoothly. Use some linking words and phrases like 'similarly' and 'on the other hand', though don't start every paragraph like this. Another strategy is to use a significant word from the last sentence of one paragraph in the first sentence of the next.

Use key terms from the topic – or synonyms for them – throughout, so the relevance of your discussion to the topic is always clear.

**The conclusion ties everything together and finishes the essay.** It includes strong statements that emphasise your central argument and provide a clear response to the topic.

Avoid simply restating the points made earlier in the essay – this will end on a very flat note and imply that you have run out of ideas and vocabulary. The conclusion is meant to be a logical extension of what you have written, not just a repetition or summary. Writing an effective conclusion can be a challenge. Try using these tips:

- Start by linking back to the final sentence of the second-last paragraph – this helps your writing to 'flow', rather than just leaping back to your main contention straight away.
- Use synonyms and expressions with equivalent meanings to vary your vocabulary. This allows you to reinforce your line of argument without being repetitive.
- When planning your essay, think of one or two broad statements or observations about the text's wider meaning. These should be related to the topic and your overall argument. Keep them for the conclusion, since they will give you something 'new' to say but still follow logically from your discussion. The introduction will be focused on the topic, but the conclusion can present a wider view of the text.

## Essay topics

1 "She has a keen, very keen, sense of the ridiculous." How do Lawson's characters find sources of humour in their grim surroundings?

2 "The boss was a mate of ours; so we stuck to him." Why do Lawson's male characters value mateship so highly?

3 "She tried to make a gentleman of me for years, but gave it up gradually." 'Although Lawson's men and women need each other, they completely fail to understand each other.' Do you agree?

4 'Lawson's characters fashion rich lives from the most meagre resources.' Discuss.

5 'The greatest difficulty Lawson's characters face is not the harshness of the bush environment, but the monotony of their lives.' Discuss.

6 'Lawson's narrators may be sympathetic to the characters they describe, but they also maintain an emotional detachment from those characters and their predicaments.' Discuss.

7 'Life in Lawson's outback has no rewards to offer.' Do you agree?

8 'Lawson's stories show that humour is the key to overcoming the difficulties of bush life.' Discuss.

9 "I could keep well away from [liquor] so long as I worked hard in the bush." 'Lawson shows that hard, physical work can triumph over both the harsh conditions of the bush, and human weakness.' Discuss.

10 "There are things that a bushwoman cannot do." 'Lawson's stories suggest that the bush is really the domain of men, not women.' Do you agree?

11 "And the sun sank again on the grand Australian bush — the nurse and tutor of eccentric minds." How do Lawson's stories suggest that the bush makes people 'eccentric'?

12 'Lawson's stories show that, although people in the bush have to work together, ultimately they are on their own.' Discuss.

## Analysing a Sample Topic

**'Lawson's stories show that humour is the key to overcoming the difficulties of bush life.' Discuss.**

The topic is of the form: 1. Contention; 2. 'Discuss' (or often: 'Do you agree?'). The term 'shows' or 'suggests' must be used in your response – as must the other key terms of the topic.

First, question the contention: *do* the stories show that humour is the key to overcoming difficulties? You might answer 'yes' (humour is the key) or 'no' (humour is not the key), or partially agree/disagree (humour is crucial, but so are other things).

Second, *how* does the text 'show' this is the case? Remember, your essay is about the ideas and values *of the text*, not your own ideas and values!

The key terms in the topic are: *humour, overcome, difficulties*. What difficulties are faced by people living in the bush (in Lawson's stories)? These could include loneliness, poverty, natural phenomena such as disease, drought, floods, fires; for women, childbirth and 'sundowners' are additional hazards.

It is immediately obvious that in Lawson's stories a sense of humour does not itself overcome these difficulties — characters are shown also to require skill, knowledge, hard work and determination, and perhaps a degree of luck. However, without a sense of humour the characters are shown to be far more vulnerable, more at risk of going mad or turning to alcohol.

This leads to a response that partially agrees/disagrees with the contention: humour is a key to survival in the bush, but other attributes are also crucial.

Evidence from the text could include:

- A 'keen sense of the ridiculous': the drover's wife, Mrs Spicer. Laughter provides relief from tears or feelings of melancholy. Joe Wilson observes: 'They had a sense of the ridiculous, most of those poor sun-dried bushwomen. I fancy that helped save them from madness.'

- A potent difficulty is loneliness; humour prevents one from taking this situation too seriously and becoming despondent and withdrawn — the 'bush undertaker' is a good example.
- Mitchell tells stories as a form of entertainment, and of reflecting on one's experiences; his yarns, such as 'Bill, the ventriloquial rooster', invest bush life with a sense of the marvellous.
- Alcohol promises relief from hardships, especially amongst male characters, but it ultimately fails as a source of solace, as is shown by the deaths of Bob Baker and Brummy 'in the horrors'; Joe Wilson says hard work, not drink is the solution.
- An extra degree of complexity in the response is generated by observing that, in Lawson's stories, difficulties are not so much overcome as confronted; humour provides a means of not being totally overwhelmed by difficulties. However, the role of humour in survival is in combination with other factors, in particular the compassion and help of one's neighbours and mates.

In your conclusion, draw together the evidence, indicating how it shows that humour is crucial to overcoming hardships. Also clarify the extent of your agreement or disagreement with the contention, perhaps qualifying your agreement by concluding that difficulties are not so much overcome as faced with the help of humour; Lawson's stories suggest that other, more practical skills and knowledges are the real 'keys' to overcoming the difficulties of bush life.

# SAMPLE ANSWER

**"It isn't bush religion to desert a mate." Why are Lawson's male characters so loyal to their mates?**

In Lawson's stories, loyalty between mates is a characteristic virtue of the male characters, a quality that they value highly in themselves and in others. This is partly a necessity of their working lives, which typically require the cooperation of two or more physically able, hard-working men. Moreover, in response to the pressures of working in isolated places, with the most basic of physical comforts, mateship also provides less tangible but equally valuable qualities, relating to the men's emotional lives and wellbeing. Their vulnerability to the elements, loneliness, alcohol and even madness is significantly reduced by the presence of a mate who is also a companion and confidant, whose loyalty will survive even death.

The need to work in teams often brings mates together; loyalty is related to the mutual need for a job to be successfully completed. In 'The Loaded Dog', Dave, Jim and Andy work together on a claim, depending on each other's talents to achieve results. For instance, Dave has the 'theories', while Andy 'put Dave's theories into practice'; Andy cooks while Dave and Jim work in the claim. This spirit of cooperation is also evident in 'Telling Mrs Baker', in which mates Jack and Andy M'Culloch are employed on a droving trip scheduled to take two years. Andy is also a mate of the boss, Bob Baker, who betrays his mates (and his family). When Bob is sacked the job has to be abandoned, emphasising the necessity of loyalty between mates through the consequences of its betrayal.

The loyalty of Andy and Jack to Bob Baker shows some of the more emotional aspects of mateship. Bob is a drinker and philanderer, and dies 'in the horrors'. Andy decides to tell a different story to Mrs Baker, which constitutes a form of loyalty to Bob's reputation as well as to his family. Jack supports this endeavour; as Andy says to Jack, 'You're surely not crawler enough to desert a mate in a case like this?' Jack observes how emotional Andy is at this time, indicating that the loyalties of mateship entail not just work skills but emotional support and sympathy, too.

Mateship loyalties take on added significance when male characters are isolated in the bush or outback, removed from the supporting structures of family and home life – structures that can provide meaning and purpose to life. An extreme instance is the old man in 'The Bush Undertaker'. His poverty and loneliness, and the harsh physical conditions in which he lives, result in his eccentric forms of behaviour. Nevertheless, mateship provides him with at least a tenuous grip on social conventions. His persistent belief in human dignity is expressed in his burial of his dead mate, Brummy. To leave Brummy's body exposed to the elements would, to him, be the equivalent of deserting a mate. Furthermore, the old man makes the improvised burial as ceremonial as possible, since ''tain't right to put 'im under like a dog'. Mateship loyalties thus extend beyond death, helping to preserve social values and rituals even in a place remote from human company and institutions.

In Lawson's stories, to 'desert a mate' is to transgress the unwritten codes of life in the bush and the outback, and earns male characters the scorn and derision of their colleagues. Yet mateship loyalties are about much more than maintaining the good opinions of one's fellow men, or harmonious working relationships. Loyalties between mates are fundamental to surviving the stresses of isolation, the temptations of alcohol and the harsh physical environment. The values, conventions and rituals of human society are sustained by mateship even in the most remote and desolate locations.

# REFERENCES & READING


## Text

Lawson, Henry, *The Penguin Henry Lawson Short Stories*, edited by John Barnes, Penguin, Ringwood, 1986.

## Australian Literature

Wilde, William H., Joy Hooton and Barry Andrews, eds., *The Oxford Companion to Australian Literature*, Oxford University Press, Melbourne, 1991.

## Australian History

Davison, Graeme, John Hirst and Stuart Macintyre, eds., *The Oxford Companion to Australian History*, revised edition, Oxford University Press, South Melbourne, 2001.

Palmer, Vance, *The Legend of the Nineties*, Melbourne University Press, Kingsgrove, 1966 (first published 1954).

## Websites

http://adb.anu.edu.au/biography/lawson-henry-7118

This site includes a detailed biography of Lawson.

https://www.sl.nsw.gov.au/stories/henry-lawson-poet-people

This site provides background material on Lawson's life and writing, including family photographs and images of some of his earliest publications and letters.